# *Isaac and Rebekah:*

## A Divine Love that defies all arranged marriage concepts!

This is book #1 of the Bible-based, historical romance novel series,

*"Love God's Way!"*

## La Wanda Blackmon

HFT PUBLISHING
Inc

**HFT Publishing, Inc**.

P. O. Box 1863

Brewton, AL 36427-1863

**Email**: HFT-Publishing@post.com

*Paperback ISBN*—978-1-953239-74-7

*eBook ISBN*—978-1-953239-75-4

Exterior and Interior Design of the book by:

*HFT Publishing, Inc.*

*limited AI text research and assistance with extensive editing*

eBook conversion by:

*HFT Publishing, Inc.*

Paperback Book Cover and eBook cover designed by:

*HFT Publishing, Inc.*

*The Cover Photo—Shutterstock photo*

# *Dedication*

To my husband, for your unwavering faith, patience, and love that mirrors the timeless devotion I sought to capture within these pages. Your presence in my life has been a testament to God's perfect timing and his boundless grace. Just as Abraham's servant was guided to find Rebekah, I was guided directly to you.

Thank you for being my constant and my greatest inspiration. Your belief in me, even when my own wavered, has been the bedrock upon which this story, and our life, was built. May our love story continue to be a reflection of the enduring power of faith and the beautiful symphony of two souls brought together by divine design.

Your steadfastness and understanding have been the quiet strength behind every word written, a silent prayer answered. This story is as much yours as it is mine, a testament to the love that guides us, sustains us, and ultimately, fulfills us. I cherish every moment with you, and I look forward to a lifetime of sharing more dreams and blessings. You are my Isaac, and I, your Rebekah, forever bound by a love that transcends time and circumstance, a love blessed from above.

"Isaac and Rebekah" by La Wanda Blackmon

# *Introduction*

There is nothing more romantic than a spell-binding historical romance based on a Bible passage. I enjoy writing these types of stories and filling in the gaps with my imagination. Call me an old-fashioned, helpless romantic. However, I classify these books as fictional Christian Romance Novels. Even though the story is true, that is in the Bible, I count it as a fictional novel because I take literary liberties to make the story an example of the wholesome love that God desires for there to be between a man and a woman, regardless of whether it is a marriage based on love, arranged marriage, or a second chance at love.

The books in the series, "***Love God's Way***," are fictional stories based on true Bible stories found in the scriptures. I list the scriptures where I found these characters in the back of this book, in the *"Reference"* section. I do not want to come across as being sacrilegious by adding to the Bible text with these stories. I am taking timeless, valuable, biblical stories and adding in the missing data based upon the customs and culture of that day. I have added this information based on my experiences living in the Middle East and working in 23 other countries throughout my nursing career.

At the time HFT Publishing, Inc. purchased this series from me, there were eight completed books and two books that were outlined and researched but not yet finished. They have made recommendations for more books. We have tossed around possible story ideas. As of the publication of this book, I have only agreed to 10 books. I will pray over this and later let my readers know if I accept the additional five books that they want for this series.

At this point in my writing, I feel that the urge for my Religious Genre writing is *"Revelation and the Last Days."* I do not feel obligated, and I do not want to feel obligated, to focus on "popular" topics to increase publication and marketing numbers. I want to remain faithful to my anointing. Once you have finished reading this book, if it has ministered to you, please add me to your prayer list and ask God to guide me in my next steps regarding writing more books for this series. I want to write to help people, and I do not want to waste any time on topics that are not beneficial.

I only agreed to this series because I had written them in the 1980s and 1990s. See the Epilogue Section for more info on when and how these books were written. To keep my Christian principles in check, I had an Assembly of God pastor and a Church of God pastor that was my "sounding boards and editors" so that I would not stray from my purpose of writing.

Because I was living in the Middle East at the time I wrote these books, and I wanted my books to be marketed to my friends and colleagues there, I aimed for readers to understand what the Torah and the Quran said about these Old Testament stories. All of these stories are covered in the Bible, the Torah, and the Quran. However, the stories vary significantly.

If a Jewish individual began reading the book and realized that the story did not match the Torah, I knew they would discard the book and never finish it. So, I had three Jewish Rabbi's that I had access to who helped me with specifics. What matches our King James Version of the Bible, I use in the story, and I explain the difference in the Epilogue under the "*Food for thought*" section.

I also had access to two very well-known Imans who had lived in Europe and the United States, who were very familiar with my Assembly of God background. I cherish the memories I have of the hours we spent debating the Bible versus the Quran during one of the most enlightening four-year periods of my life. Like with the Torah, the Quran differences are covered in the "*Food for Thought*" section.

I am not trying to make this series a Christian-Jewish-Muslim love series. I want my readers to understand that up front. This is a Christian romance series based on Biblical stories from the Old Testament. (Some from the New Testament may be added later if the publisher and editor get their wishes.) But the info from the Torah and the Quran is listed to help keep the Jews and Muslims from being confused about what I am writing. It is also there to keep my Christian readers aware of customs not like theirs. We all need to learn from each other.

The day that we as Christians stop learning and we stop respecting other faiths and cultures, that is the day we lose the love of Jesus Christ that our faith is built upon. That is the day that we need to either change or take down the sign that says we are Christians.

7

I want all of my readers to know that I have shaped these stories to promote the Judeo-Christian values of a wholesome woman, as described in the King James version of **Proverbs 31** by King Solomon in the Bible. Some of the other translations change the purpose and focus of this awesome book written by King Solomon.

By adding this content, I can make these historical romantic stories relevant to the 21st Century. As a nation, we have lost our love for teaching and training our children. We have let the schools, their peers, and the "Hollywood" scene teach our children what they need to know about love, sex, and marriage. That was not God's plan.

If I can help a young man or woman realize what God wants from them—to be a consecrated bride—then all the time and research I have invested in writing these books will be worth it. My primary purpose for writing these types of stories is to give the young people of this generation an idea of how God intended love to be celebrated.

Most of our children have only experienced love through the lens of Hollywood, with its sinful actions and innuendos, or the works of the flesh. I want our children and my grandchildren to experience love like God intended.

I also want them to have something wholesome to put into their minds and hearts. Instead of unbridled sex, lust, drugs, alcohol, and rebellion to or resistance of authority, I want them to desire to obey God. I want my grandsons to have a wholesome love for their wives and my granddaughters to grow up to be Proverbs 31 women.

I pray that all of my readers will see that the Bible tells stories and writes awesome love letters to us. Our heavenly father used parables and stories to give us a pattern or example of true love, not a demon-possessed, drug-popping, drinking, partying extrovert or sexual deviant as a role model.

Join me for the timeless story of Issac and Rebekah. Then next month you can join me for the love triangle of Jacob, Rachel, and Leah!

Enjoy and God Bless!

*La Wanda Blackmon*

*P.S. Carol, my dear friend and Editor, you pushed me to let this series get published. Thank you for helping me let go of years of rejection over this series and giving HFT Publishing a chance. The success of this series is not because I was listening to God's small inner voice. It was you who was listening and started tormenting me to let this series go to press. Without you, the world would have never known the beautiful stories written so many, many years ago when I lived in the Middle East, where I could research them myself! Thanks for listening to our Heavenly Father!*

## <u>Chapter One:</u>

# *God's Plan for how to find a wife for Isaac*

The weight of a promise God had given to Abraham that his descendants would be as numerous as the sand settled upon Eliezer, like the dust of the Gaza hillside, as Abraham was talking to him this morning. What a family burden, spiritual burden, and impossible task Abraham was asking of him.

Eliezer was Abraham's Chief Servant and head of his household. Eliezer would have been Abraham's heir if Isaac had not been born. Eliezer was from Damascus, Syria. When Eliezer woke that morning, he had no idea that he would be traveling to see Nahor (Abraham's brother) in the village of Ur in Mesopotamia. (Modern-day Iraq).

The village where Nahor and Abraham were raised was in the highly fertile lands that lay between the Tigris and Euphrates Rivers. (In the Bible, it is classified as Ur, the land of the Chaldeans. This was an area that the Syrians, Iraqis, and Turkish merchants and inhabitants still influence today. It is some of the most beautiful land on earth.)

When Abraham finished explaining to Eliezer this impossible task to find the perfect wife for Isaac and this heritage Abraham would be leaving him, Eliezer instructed the managing servants to feed, water, and saddle up 10 camels, plus the carts (carriage like carriers) that they used for the women to sleep in when they stopped to make camp along the way at night.

Eliezer's mind was going wild. He was making a mental to-do list, and Abraham was still talking. Eliezer is thinking, "Why do all of these old men have to keep rattling on and on? Why can't they let me take a few commands at a time and disperse them out, then give me more? It would not do me any good to write them down; the servants cannot read. I have to give them tasks one at a time, or they will forget! Oh, God, I am too stressed this morning. Please do not let him get mad when I tell him to shut up—give me wisdom on how to handle him. If I do not say something, he is going to get mad when I make a flop of this assignment." Eliezer was praying silently.

He looked up from his prayer; he was camouflaging while we were tightening the strap on his sandals. "You did not hear a word I just said, did you?" Abraham said with a sharp and raspy voice.

"Yes, I heard you, but you have got to slow down, you are so excited and talking so fast, I cannot remember what you are saying, so how am I going to relay this to the servants? Successfully, anyway!"

12

Abraham blushed. "I get this way every time Yahweh speaks to me. I am sorry. Let me get you a couple of tablets. I will create a list for you to pack for this trip, including instructions on where to go and who to contact, as well as a third list with the instructions for making the covenant with the new bride. Oh, yeah, I almost forgot. The four tablets will require a list of items to be taken for the bride, her family, and to make the covenant/contract legal in Ur. I will send a fifth sack of money with you (you will not need a tablet to know what to do or purchase to come back—you will simply return with the same items that you took with you to go to Ur). This fifth sack of money will be for purchasing the items you will need for the return trip."

"Okay. That is a plan. Can you please give me a minute to eat breakfast with my wife and explain to her that I will be leaving soon to go away?" Eliezer said with an urgent plea in his voice.

"I am sorry, by all means, eat. You will need your energy. But the trip will not be soon. You will pack and get ready today and leave at first light in the morning!" Abraham said with that excited ramble coming back to his voice!

Eliezer turned to go to the cooking pot outside their tent. He could hear his wife calling him. Out of the corner of his eye, he saw his youngest son running toward him. Chaos was about to kick in; he needed to get away from Abraham before this kid arrived, or his master would think that he was incapable of handling a trip of such importance.

When Abraham realized Eliezer was about to walk away, he shouted, "Don't think I won't remember where we need to start. I have to tell you what God said, and then I will share with you the long history of my family. You have to know all of the drama and what to expect, or you will bring back the wrong wife for Isaac!"

Eliezer threw his hand up as he walked away in a "yes, I got you" manner. While muttering under his breath, "God, I hope you are up and ready for this—because I am not—you've got to give me strength to make it through today successfully, because I cannot fail on this trip! It would be okay if you want to send those three Angels that came to talk to Abraham when Sarah was pregnant—send them. That will be okay. Someone has got to do something now! I know that Abraham and my father were close to the same age. I know that I was born after my father came to be Abraham's servant. I am much older than Ishmael (Abraham's son by his wife's slave, Hagar) and Isaac. I am gray-headed and starting to show my years. I am not the 25-year-old spring chicken that took my father's place when he died. You have to help Abraham understand this and help my wife be patient enough to make it through these next four months. Please, please God!" Eliezar shuddered and grunted as he reached to pull back the opening in the tent to see if his wife was in there.

When he completed this prayer, a calmness washed over him like a gentle rain. He was grateful for the confirmation from God that his prayer would be answered.

Before he could finish his conversation with his wife, which he was going to be an hour later than he originally planned, someone touched Eliezer's shoulder with a firm grip. Eliezer almost jumped out of his skin. He had no idea that anyone was near enough to hear his conversation with his wife, much less touch him.

It was Abraham. "One more thing, I want you and your family to join me for dinner tonight. I need to discuss all of this 'family stuff' with you and prepare you mentally for this trip. You have to know what God showed me in the early hours this morning. So can I expect you at sundown?"

14

Eliezer moaned and shook his head no, much to Abraham's shock. He had not expected a rapid rejection from his servant. It was always an honor to eat with Abraham and Isaac.

Then Eliezer began to explain that he wanted a quiet evening with his wife, as this would be the last one for about four months. Abraham nodded that he understood. Then, to Eliezer's wife's surprise, Abraham offered an unexpected compromise.

"Well, that is fine. I will join you while you are having your supper. I will not eat, that will be too early for me. But I will talk while you and your family are eating. Your wife, sons, daughters, and in-laws need to know the full story. Someday, one of them will be taking over for you when you are gone. They need to know how to help Isaac. He will be the one in charge then. So, I will be the entertainment this afternoon!"

As Eliezer looked up, he saw such a look of shock on his wife's face that he thought she was going to pass out. His daughter was nearby, so he whispered to her to gather her sisters and all the daughters-in-law and inform them of what was happening. His wife was going to need reinforcements. This meant that 63 more people would be joining them for early supper. Not the 14 that his wife was accustomed to preparing the evening meal for—but all 77 people needed to hear this legacy from Abraham's mouth!

Eliezer had not realized how big his family had gotten until he went to pull together seating arrangements for them all. He decided that the best way to arrange the tables was to move some stones that were close by, which would quickly be thick enough to make the tables high enough to get their legs and knees under while those who sat on the ground. He could lay some timbers from the work area where the servants, who were skilled carpenters, had been working for the last three weeks, building the new barn where they could shelter the goats during a storm. The goats and sheep fought too much each time they were put in the same building (open concept barn style building).

Once they scattered them around, he realized that Abraham's voice was probably not loud enough for the people at the back tables to hear the details, especially if a baby or toddler was going to be at that table. So, he began arranging the stones in a large square. He left enough space between two of the tables on one side where Abraham could get in the middle and talk. He also stood some wooden crates on their ends so that the servants could temporarily place food and trays on them as they served his family. The servants could also work from inside the square as well as from the outside.

As soon as this square table configuration was in place, he looked at the three sons helping him and said, "Now, go to your mother. Do whatever she tells you. Tonight is going to be better than attending a theater drama in Alexandra, Egypt! This is probably a once-in-a-lifetime event!"

With that word of instruction, Eliezer was off to the fields where the lambs and goats were being kept by one of the shepherds. He had to decide how many he needed to take with him to feed his 10-camel caravan of workers for the initial four to five weeks of travel to their destination. Abraham had already selected the cattle and lambs that would be part of the gifts to the bride's family. Those animals had been tagged and a marking made in their flesh on the right hip flank so that they would not accidentally kill one of the "gift animals."

About halfway to this grazing area, it hit Eliezer— a strange but familiar feeling. It was a burden that he had carried for years since he had taken over his father's position as Chief Steward for Abraham. Today, it felt like this burden was a mantle woven from threads of loyalty, faith, and an unspoken covenant between himself and his master, and blessed by their God, Yahweh!

Finally, it was time for this strange afternoon meal, and entertainment from their Master had arrived. Each of Eliezer's family members began taking their seats, as instructed by Eliezer and his wife. They all had so many questions.

Eliezer kept saying, "Be patient, you will see what this is about in about half an hour. Master Abraham is going to share with us his life, his legacy, and what God asked of him. We have all heard the myths and legends shared among the servants, and occasionally, we hear a local merchant tell us something about Abraham that we did not know. But tonight, we are going to hear it from Abraham himself. No guesswork, no drawn conclusions, no GPAs in the story, and no assumptions. It is going to be awesome. Now sit down, be quiet, and be respectful. Abraham is getting on in years; he rambles almost as much as your grandfather did before he died. This will probably be the last, and definitely the only time that Abraham will have to tell us this story—his story!"

## Chapter Two:

# *The History of Abraham*

The sun was getting ready to start its descent. It would be hours before it set. It had been a long three days since Abraham had turned his life and the entire compound upside down. That was the first day of the week when Abraham came to the woodpile, where Eliezer was trying to chop some wood into small pieces that his wife could use under the old iron cookpot. Abraham was so excited and rambling on like a thunderstorm threatening to take their homes away.

Now, three days later, he was finally seeing everything packed and tied onto the camels. He could see the sun getting ready to set. His wife would have his supper ready in a few minutes. He had told her it needed to be at the beginning of the sun to start its daily descent (around 4 pm by our standards) today, instead of waiting until it was dark. It was midsummer. There was so much work to do in the fields that they would often wait until way after dark to eat during the summer. (This would be around 9 pm by our standards now).

While he was checking the four tablets of goods he had prepared for packing, he had a sense of satisfaction sweep over him as he realized that he was almost done. Then he laughed as he remembered Abraham saying on the first day that he would make a tablet with a list of the things he needed to pack for the journey he would take the next morning. Now, three days later, he was still packing. The initial packing tablet was not one but four!

As he was laughing, his wife walked up asking what was so funny. He reached out, grabbed her, and pulled her close. As he squeezed her, he planted a kiss on her forehead. "My dear one, I was just thinking how much like a woman Abraham has become in his old age. He said we would pack and leave the next morning. Three days later, we are still packing. We transitioned from a single tablet list to four lists for this journey. I have not even started on the list of gifts for the bride and her family! I hope I am ready for supper early as we planned. I want to have plenty of time for rest before dawn and lots of private time with you, my dear one. It will probably be four months before I see you again. I do not know if I can be gone from you that long. At least I will have this evening to think about each night when I try to sleep on the ground!"

She kissed him back and said, "Eliezar, I love you, but sometimes you get so lost in work that it is not healthy. I came to remind you that Abraham is coming to talk to us tonight while we eat. If you still have some more checking to do, you will have to do it after he leaves. You cannot afford to be late. Do I need to send one of the boys to help you wrap this up?"

Eliezar laughed and said, "No. You know how I am. I always double-check and sometimes triple-check everything. I am through. Hold on, and I will walk back with you. I can smell the food all the way out here. I think you may have overdone this meal. But I am grateful, since I will be on the road for so long without your wonderful cooking."

As Eliezer and his wife came walking up to the "square seating center" that he and his sons had designed earlier. He looked up, and Abraham and Isaac were coming around the corner of their tent. He had arrived just in time!

Eliezer quickly got everyone seated and instructed the servants to begin serving the appetizers, then to proceed with the other courses of the meal without hesitation. He explained that their guest would need some wine and water, but they would be speaking while the family ate. The servants looked puzzled. A couple of them frowned and shook their heads in disbelief, but moved forward.

Abraham stepped into the center of the square of tables and motioned for Isaac to bring a large chunk of wood into the center for him to sit on.

"As most of you know," Abraham started, "Sarah and I were ancient when Issac was born. It was a divine miracle that we had him. I was already 75 years old when God first promised me that he would give me a son. I was just arriving here in Canaan. God told me that my descendants would be like the stars of the heavens and the sands of the sea—impossible to count. However, that promise was not fulfilled until Sarah was ninety and I was one hundred years old. So today I stand before you, 140 years old, and Isaac is 39."

As he was taking a sip of water, Eliezer's youngest grandson chirped out, "Gee, you are really old. You are old like God!" Everyone broke out laughing as they looked at little Eli, who was gesturing with his hands how an old man walked.

That was the best "icebreaker" that could have been used for any meeting. It was like the laughter gave Abraham a burst of energy. He forgot how tired he was; he went wide open into Pentecostal Pastor mode as he decided to recount the whole story.

Then Isaac continued to explain, "Well, let me back up some more. Before I provide you with any more information about the journey you are about to take, I would like to share with you, Eliezer, my own history. That is why I agreed to share it tonight while you were all eating. All of you need to know our heritage. What God did for me, he did for you, too. You are all a part of my family. You are all my heirs, too! I know that God is the reason why I am here today. I appreciate the fact that God used all of you to help me on my journey. So, it is only right for you to know your legacy."

Abraham took a deep breath and continued, "I was 75 years old when Sarah and I arrived here in this area (Canaan). We were here 25 years when God sent angels to tell me that he was going to honor me with a son from my loins with Sarah. I was 100 years old and Sarah was 90 years old when Isaac was born."

"Not only was I not born and raised here, but my ancestral heritage is not one that was dedicated to Yahweh. So, I am going to take you on a historical journey. My father was Shem, and my grandfather was Noah. God promised me that I would be the father of many nations. I realize that the promise appears to be mute, considering that I am already 140 years old now. However, my Father, Terah, and my grandfather Nahor, who lived in Ur of the Chaldeans (modern-day Tell el-Muqayyar in southern Iraq—located approximately 160 kilometers north-west of Basra) when I was born. I grew up in this ancient city, situated on the western bank of the Euphrates River. Tell el-Muqayyar was near Nasiriyah (the Baghdad Eyalet of the Ottoman Empire—Now Baghdad, Iraq)."

Abraham stopped to drink some wine, shifted on the log, and began again. "See, my grandfather Nahor was the son of Serug, who was a descendant of Shem, one of Noah's sons who was saved on the ark with Noah. My grandfather was only 29 years old when my father, Terah, was born. However, my father, Terah, was 70 years old before he had my two brothers and me."

Isaac spoke up and said, "Do not forget to tell them about your brothers, Dad." Abraham continued, "I had two brothers in Nahor, named after my grandfather, and Haran. Haran was Lot's father. My father was 70 when I was born. I was 75 when I arrived here, and my dad was 145 years old. He did not come with me but stayed in Nahor. He could not accept my one God; he needed many to worship to keep his merchants happy.

Considering I am currently 140 years old, that would make my father 210 years old if he were still alive. I found out from a messenger three years ago that my dad died in Harran at the age of 205. I pray I live that long!"

"I came from a long line of idol worshippers. When God spoke to me, my family thought I was delusional. They could not accept the fact that there was only one God. They tried to get me not to leave. But I shared with Sarah what God had shared with me, and she agreed with me that I had to follow God—the one true God—Yahweh. So here we are!"

Then Abraham begins to give Issac's life timeline. "Isaac was born when Sarah was 90 years old, and I was 100 years old. When God tested me to see if I would give him my only son, Issac was 26 years old. Sarah was 127 years old when she died. I was 137 years old and Issac was 37 at the time of her death. Isaac is now 39. He will be 40 before you can get back here with a wife for him. His life is just beginning. I am getting older. Some days I do not feel that I will make 200 like my father. So, I must ensure that Issac has a strong support system and family to back him. I have to know that you, Eliezer, understand what is going on. I need you to instill in your son what I have shared with you for the past 75 years. I have to know that my legacy will not go away and that my son will not be swayed to go the way of his grandfather and worship idols!"

Eliezer looked up from his plate and saw that Abraham was crying. He was not sure how long that steady flow of tears had been coming down his face, because his voice had not broken. At that moment, Eliezer made a promise to God to see that every word of Abraham is fulfilled.

After finishing his glass of wine, Abraham continued. "I need you to know what land was promised to my descendants. Please make note of these areas. We have to keep ownership of these areas secured."

"The land God promised me," Abraham explained, "stretched from the southern border near Kadesh-Barnea to the 'torrent valley of Egypt' (Adi el-Arish and includes areas to the north, such as Mount Hor and Lebo-Hamath. The eastern boundary ran along the Jordan River, encompassing much of Modern-day Israel and its surrounding territories. Our land encompasses the Mediterranean coastal plain in the west and the southern desert, near here (Gaza), as well as parts of the Dead Sea region. It stretches up to the Jordan Valley. However, the Jordan Valley, Sodom, and Gomorrah are not part of this core section we call Canaan."

He continues, "When we arrived here in Canaan, it was sparsely settled. That is why we have so much grazing land. The villages or tribal camps were basically concentrated along the Mediterranean coast, the Dead Sea basin, and the fertile plains of Jezreel and the Jordan Valley. I personally chose this hill country and allowed Lot to have the fertile plains near Sodom. In comparison, I had several reasons for choosing the hill country. But my main purpose was that it was largely unoccupied. I would not have to fight to take the land, and I would have plenty of grazing areas."

The servants were through cleaning up their plates and bowls. So, Eliezer recommended that they move over to the campfire. The kids could sit on the ground. That would give Eliezer and Abraham more comfortable places to sit.

"When God spoke to me," Abraham continued after getting settled onto the quilted bed and pillows behind his back, "He gave me instructions to come here, and I obeyed without questioning him. I felt peace as soon as he spoke to me. When I arrived here, I offered a sacrifice to God. When I did, he spoke to me and said, 'Abraham, lift up your eyes and look from the place where you are, northward, southward, eastward, and westward, for all the land that you see I will give to you and to your offspring forever.' Oh, my what a promise that was! I was excited, but then remembered I did not have an heir to leave it to. So, I prayed!"

"Now, I want you, Eliezer," Abraham said with authority, "and any of your family or other servants that you select to go with you on this trip to know why this is so important for me. I must have a wife for my son, Isaac, who is not from the Canaanite women or anyone who had been contaminated with pagan worship as a temple priestess. I am looking for a young lady who is still pure and has a deep love for God. If she is not aware of Yahweh, she will need to be someone who will convert

25

and agree to serve only the one God, Yahweh, for the rest of her life."

Eliezar could feel the air, even though the sun was setting in the west and was almost gone. The air still felt thick with the heat of the hot summer desert, and everyone and all animals smelled of this stench that you couldn't get rid of until dark each day. Most evenings by this time, he would come in to eat, then go to the tent out back and strip down to bathe. Tonight, he was sitting here listening to Abraham—something he would have never dreamed would happen.

He looked at the pile of old stones about 50 feet from Abraham, which was still there as a witness that Abraham had not allowed idols or high places, for his jealous God would only allow worship of Him. That pile of stones had been an altar base for an idol of Baal. As he looked at that pile of rocks, he found himself wondering how many times those stones had witnessed the rise and fall of prophets, kings, merchants, priests, and other wealthy individuals, just as they had witnessed God's plans for Abraham and Isaac that night.

It was as if Eliezer could feel the quiet anticipation of everyone, including the stones, for what was about to come to this compound, the villages, and the surrounding cities in the years to come. He also felt the heaviness of the task ahead of him and what it would mean to Abraham and Isaac if he failed this assignment.

Then Eliezer's attention was drawn back to Abraham, his face etched with the wisdom of age and the deepening shadows of mortality, who had summoned Isaac to his side to help him get up. At 140 years of age, he was too feeble to walk around in the dark without someone holding on to him. He did not need a broken hip or leg, or worse, a snake bite!

Everyone around the campfire commented after Abraham and Isaac left on how this patriarch's voice, though frail, still carried the resonance of authority and the unwavering conviction of a man who walked closely with and communed frequently with Yahweh.

"Now, off to bed with all of you," Eliezer bellowed out, "dawn comes early. We must be up and ready to leave at first light. We cannot afford to lose one minute of daylight on this journey. I am certain that Abraham will not sleep tonight for more than a couple of hours. He will be up and ready, waiting for us in the morning. He will be inspecting things, asking questions, and hindering us. So, being punctual is important. Do you understand?" Everyone nodded in agreement as they got up and cleared away the mess they had made. Then everyone was off to their tents or huts.

Eliezer knew it would be hard for him to sleep. So, as he walked to his tent with his arm around his wife's shoulders, he was praying for God to intervene and give him a good night's rest!

## Chapter Three:

# *Day One—Journey to Ur*

Something was going on. There was something in the compound that did not belong here. Eliezer was awakened from a deep sleep by the baying of four dogs and the early morning roosters sounding their wake-up call, which began over an hour before sunrise. Two of the shepherds were running toward him as he stepped outside his tent, "Eliezer, a lion was stalking us. We moved the sheep back to the compound. Just as we got them locked in the sheepfold, the dogs started barking furiously. I think the lion must have followed us here. Come quickly,

29

we cannot afford to have our flock and children lost to this beast!"

Eliezer thought to himself that this was a peculiar way to wake up, but he was grateful that they could deal with this before he left and not have to worry about it attacking while he was away. So, he said a silent prayer, asking Yahweh to anoint them that morning. He barked out instructions to everyone he passed on his way to meet the armed warriors that Abraham kept on guard at all times. Eliezer might be in lion-trapping mode, but he wanted that caravan ready before Abraham got up!

To the amazement of the guards and Eliezer, the lion was right where the shepherds said it would be. He was very old and walked with a limp. He had probably been injured in a fight with a younger male lion for his pride. This old king was probably no longer allowed in the pride's camp or den. So, he had to hunt prey that was easier to get. It did not take these mighty warriors but a few minutes to have enough arrows in this lion to put him down. They quickly cut his head off. They would drag the carcass back to the camp and dispose of it after the caravan had left. However, they did not want to attract wild dogs and other beasts with the smell of the blood, so they moved it. They would deal with it soon.

Eliezer was packed, hugging everyone goodbye, and about 50 feet from the camel he was going to mount when he heard Abraham's voice.

"Eliezer," he began bellowing, his gaze piercing, yet his voice was filled with a profound tenderness, "you have been my most trusted servant. You know my heart, and you know the promises God has made to me and my descendants. Now, I am old, and it is getting close to my time to depart from this world. Before I go, as I explained last night, there is one final task I must entrust to you. I know you are almost as old as I am. But you are healthier. So, I want to remind you this morning of the urgency— do not drag around getting to Ur and hurry back to me.

There is one thing I forgot to tell you last night. You know that here on this compound, when we make a marriage covenant, we try to select a girl between the ages of 12 and 14. We marry her to the man we have selected between 14 and 16, depending upon her physical and mental development. There is a reason—the older they are, the more likely they are not to be pure or may never accept our God. So, make sure you keep this in mind when you are looking. Be cautious of the girl's age and upbringing. Now, off with you! I will be praying daily until you return!"

With those last words, he gave Eliezer and two of his sons who were accompanying him a bear hug and a kiss on each cheek. Eliezer could hear his heart beating loudly in his chest. This was not a dream, even though the last four days had been a blur since Abraham ran into the compound saying God had spoken to him on the mount.

This was not going to a mire wife selecting trip. This was a covenantal act, a crucial step in fulfilling the promise Yahweh had made to Abraham almost 70 years ago. It was a promise that would still be producing results thousands of years in the future. He had to get it right! Eliezer had watched Isaac grow from the day he was born until now. He knew that he could describe his master and his son without difficulty. He also knew that he could select the proper wife if Yahweh would anoint him, as he had when he and Abraham pursued the kings who tried to take Sodom over and captured Lot and his family.

As Eliezer went to give his wife one final hug and kiss, she squeezed him tightly and whispered into his ear. "Eliezer, remember you are not to seek a bride from the daughters of Ur that are like the daughters of Canaan and the surrounding areas. Fleeting customs, worldly desires, and wealth can easily sway those girls. Please do not display the gifts or mention them until you are certain you have the right candidate. Some women can be anything you want them to be to get the gold. They can be perfect for a couple of weeks, then their claws come out! Remember the Heritage Abraham shared with us last night. Think about this the entire trip, and your mind will be in the right place when you arrive. I know that Yahweh will guide you with wisdom that is not your own, because only Yahweh knows the tapestry he is making. We only see the under, ugly side. The weaver sees the top. God's grand design will be perfect. Just trust Yahweh and that small still voice the entire trip in all things, including safety and dealings with people in the towns you go through.

As Eliezer's wife was finishing her last hug, they both heard Abraham's voice again. He was telling everyone to load up and get going because the sun was peaking over the horizon. Get going. The quicker you leave and the faster you travel, the quicker you will return with my future daughter-in-law. I cannot rest until this task is completed. God's urgency is not to be avoided or extended.

Eliezer and the ten camel caravan begin to pull out. He has to go southwest when he leaves the compound, as if he is heading to Gaza and then to Egypt. That is not the direction they are headed, but that is the only way to get out of this area safely and not go through the mountain passes where the vagabonds attack richly laden caravans.

Eliezer knew all the best paths around the entire southern area, from Gaza and the Mediterranean Sea to the border lands, and all the way to the Euphrates River. However, some of those paths were not safe when women traveled with you overnight.

Their journey would not be a direct northeastern track toward the Jordan Valley and through the forest of Lebanon. They would take a much safer winding path through well-inhabited areas and cities, where supplies could be secured. Then they went through Shechem and over to Damascus. The navigation through Syria toward the Euphrates River was going to be a long, winding path as they got to the hill country. Then it became risky as they approached the borderlands. He had been to the edge but no further. He had no idea what they would encounter in Lebanon. He had no idea where would be best to cross the Euphrates River. The Path that Abraham took through Haran when he came here years ago was not safe. It may be better now. He would have to investigate all of this when he reached those areas.

He would have to send a messenger ahead of him once he got close to the Euphrates River to see if the caravan would need to go to Heran, Nahor, or Ur. Abraham had no idea where his brothers were residing now that their father was dead. Communication by messages or scrolls given to someone on a caravan took months, sometimes a year, to reach you. Occasionally, the caravans were robbed, and the messages never reached their destinations. So, he had no idea where Abraham's family was currently residing. But he was certain God knew, and he would direct them.

Oh, so much to think about, so much to do before selecting a wife for Isaac. Eliezer was getting tired just rehearsing the "to-do list" Abraham had given him. Eliezer had already experienced moments where the thoughts of this journey were overwhelming to him before he left the compound this morning. He had to focus on his journey, not miss any landmarks or forget any tasks. So, he scolded himself for letting his mind wander.

"Eliezer, get a grip," he told himself, "You know the mission, the task, and what to look for. You are close to Abraham and Isaac. Choosing for them would be easy for you!" Eliezer had endured numerous trials and tests with Abraham. He had experienced Abraham's unwavering faith firsthand. He needed to prepare himself mentally, just as he had physically when packing the camels.

33

Eliezer made a mental note to himself to find the scroll that contained all the things God had told Abraham. He would take it out and read it each night. That would surely keep him focused on the promises God made to Abraham and Sarah. He would read it and pray for wisdom, anointing, and discernment. He would ask God to help him find a woman of kindness, integrity, and faithfulness. The woman he chose for Isaac would need to possess similar traits, such as a gentle heart, a resilient spirit, and a faith that leaned on Yahweh for everything while serving Him with complete devotion.

As Eliezer looked out over the sprawling hills, the landscape appeared to be bathed in the soft glow of the rising sun, and he felt a surge of purpose. This was not merely a quest for a bride; it was a sacred mission, a delicate thread in the grand tapestry of God's plan, and he was ready to carry its weight. He understood that selecting a life partner, especially one destined to be part of such a divinely orchestrated lineage, was a decision that required more than human wisdom; it demanded divine guidance, a reliance on faith that transcended all earthly considerations. He placed his trust not in his own capabilities, but in the One who had called Abraham, yes, Yahweh, the God of Abraham, believing that He would lead his steps to the one chosen to be a wife for his master's son.

They had reached the place where he had hoped they would be able to camp the first night away. They were only 15 miles from Gaza. He had hoped that they would be able to travel 20 miles per day. However, he only hoped to make 15 miles the first day. He was padding his itinerary in case there were any delays in leaving that morning. They had actually arrived at this spot a couple of hours early. He dared not try to push forward for two more hours because he was not certain where they would camp. He had been this way before, so he knew about this place. It was better to stay safe. He would rather err on the side of caution than put the women with him at risk.

As he lay his head down on his folded tunic and stretched out on the blanket his wife had packed for him, he remembered thinking, I never knew a blanket on the ground could feel so good. I cannot remember where I put the bedding roll. I will locate it in the morning. I can have a more comfortable night tomorrow night. I am so tired that I think I could sleep standing up, he thought.

Just as his head hit the tunic, his heavy eye came wide awake. Sleep left his mind, and the heavy weight of Abraham's promise and the responsibility of this trip rushed into his mind. It was not a burden of dread, but a solemn consecration. Eliezer knew he had packed the provisions, the fine linens, the precious metals that would serve as tokens of his master's generosity, and the future that awaited them, along with all the things they would need on this trip. He had followed Abraham's list perfectly. But he was over a hundred years old himself. What if he forgot something? What would happen? It was the weight of history, the weight of destiny, and the profound responsibility of ensuring that Isaac's lineage would continue according to the divine mandate and Abraham's instructions that had been bugging his mind.

He closed his eyes, whispered a prayer to Yahweh, asking for relaxation, sleep to come, protection, and a refreshed wakefulness in the morning. To his amazement, he immediately fell asleep.

**The end of the first week:**

As the sun climbed higher, casting long shadows across the ancient landscape, Eliezer mounted his camel, his heart steady, his gaze fixed on the horizon. The mission was well underway. They had been traveling for eight days now. This was the first day of the second week. The heat was about to do them in today. He had never been so tired or ached so much. "God, he prayed, please grant me enduring strength to make this quest, the humility and patience to wait on you, and the ability to rely on the revelation of your divine will. Bless this journey from this through to its completion."

Eliezer' camel rose, rocking and a peace fell over the entire caravan as if to let everyone on this journey know that they were all carrying a sacred vow, a testament to Abraham's enduring faith, stepping out from the heart of an ancient land into a future yet to be revealed, guided by the whisper of a promise that had echoed through time. He was so grateful that they were only three miles from where he had planned to camp for tonight, according to the rug merchant at the souk they had just stopped at. They also ate while they were there. That would help tonight. They would not have to set up for cooking supper. They could make camp and prepare for the morning meal.

About a half mile from the souk, Eliezer began to hear sheep bleating. It reminded him of the sounds that had sung "goodbye and return quickly" to them as they were leaving Gaza. They had ridden passed the pastures where Abraham's shepherd were grazing the sheep and cattle and moved toward the town part of their village, the sounds of early vendors setting up their stalls, the distant bleating of sheep, and the murmur of prayers from his fellow servants were all too familiar to Eliezer, who had been in Abrahams employe now for more than seventy years. That sound was reassuring when they left. This afternoon, it was hauntingly nostalgic.

Even though he had heard these sounds almost every day, they felt different and more pronounced today. They were imbued with a significance that transcended the ordinary. He had made it a week; he had reached a landmark. Then his thoughts went crazy. What if I am

36

not successful? What if I find the perfect girl and she refuses to leave her parents? Can I bring them? What if they refuse to come? I brought female servants to take care of her and protect her. I should have brought my two daughters. One is twelve and the other is 14. Even though both are already betrothed, I may have pleaded with their husband. It would only be four months of the year-long process that they would be away, and they would have been with me, their dad—what could be safer? Why didn't I think of this before now? Guess I will have to convince a couple of her friends to travel with her, so she will not be lonely.

Then just as quickly as the rush of questions flooded his mind, they stopped. He thanked God and said, "Yahweh, you are too good to me. You have stopped Satan from tormenting me based on one simple prayer. Now I ask you for something that I probably do not deserve—rest tonight for all of us, renewal of our strength. I invite you to work on the people at the other end of my journey. Soften them up for me, please God!

As they top the hill, Eliezer sees the plateau ahead, where they will camp. He calls out to his male servants. Everyone gets excited. Another day has passed without complications, with no one falling ill and no tragic events.

## The last day of week two:

As the sun began to rise, the camp was in an uproar. Everyone was running in all directions. It seems that Yahweh had answered Eliezer's prayer for a great night of rest for everyone, because everyone overslept. So, they were all fighting to make up for lost time.

When Eliezer realized what had happened, he called all of them to gather around him. "Calm down," he said, "We all overslept by one hour. Yahweh saw that we needed it. He will anoint us today. If you rush, we may leave something valuable behind or make a mistake in packing that could put someone's life at risk. Slow down, do the job right. No stress. I am certain that we will be able to make up the hour later today."

With that, everyone slowed down, and the chaos began to disappear. The ride was smooth for the next four hours. Then they made a quick stop to tie down some blankets that were trying to fly away.

Several servants had questions about the animals before Eliezer could remount his camel. He knew that the initial stages of this journey would take weeks, but now the tiredness of being on the road for so long was catching up with them all. They had travelled each day since they left. Tomorrow would be the day they would rest from work and offer a sacrifice to Yahweh if they were back on the compound. So, Eliezer decided that not only did his staff need a rest, but he also felt that the animals would benefit. When he told them that they would rest tomorrow, the look of relief settled on all of them. He would explain to them all, once they had set up camp, that the next day would be a day of worship. He felt that Yahweh would honor this. He was shocked that he had not thought about this before tonight.

## The day of rest and worship:

Eliezer lazily lay on his bedroll with the blanket wrapped over him. It had gotten cool here last night. It was the mountain air coming in from the north and the clouds blowing in from the east. As he looked at the sky, he knew why Yahweh Had had them stop. Today would not have been a day for travel. The weather was going to be rainy and stormy.

He had everyone pack their bedding and put it in the carriages to protect them from the rain. Eliezer found an Inn with a shop attached where they could buy already-cooked food that was hot, not snacks. They hunkered down for the day, where it would be dry.

Eliezer sat there, staring out at the rain, thinking about how at each place where they stopped to buy food, water the camels, or spend the night, everyone in the caravan added to the many memories that they would later remember and cherish. The land itself seemed to whisper tales of ages past. The valleys had been carved by time and weather, passed by rocky outcrops that had witnessed the passage of countless caravans, he was certain. This journey had been incredible. This day of rest, along with the protection it offered from the storm, was another miracle and memory to add to the list of things they would share with Abraham and Isaac when they returned to Canaan.

### The morning after the first day of rest:

They had averaged around 20 miles per day so far after that first day. Even with the day of rest today, they were still on schedule. However, Eliezer knew that, over the next 10 or 12 days, the terrain for the next week would be more challenging, and they would only make 12-15 miles per day. Eliezer was quickly trying to calculate that he would have to travel at least 900 miles.

Depending on where in Ur he could find a wife for Issac, he might have to go further into Mesopotamia, making his trip upwards of 1,100 to 1,400 miles. "Oh God, please bless me, and send me the right woman at Ur. With a minimum of four weeks to get there, a couple of weeks at the place in preparation to return for another four- or five-week journey, God, I will be on the road for about 90 days. The longer we are on the road, the greater our risk becomes. Please give us safety and protection. Part the weather for us and prevent delays. We ask this in the name of our master, Abraham!"

This area of the world was constantly in flux. The traveling merchants always bring their idols and pleasures of other regions to try to entice the people of Canaan. The constant ministering that was necessary for Abraham to help keep his family and servants anchored to the promises God made to Abraham and not swayed by idol worship was a full-time job for his Master. It seems that evil is always present, trying to stop good.

Eliezer carried this anchor, Abraham's words of warning, within him as he ventured forth. His mission, though rooted in the ancient past, was undeniably directed toward the future—a future that would be shaped by the choices made and the paths that would now be taken.

There had not been a grand announcement or party before their departure. There had been no fanfare. As Eliezer's pulse was beating to the rhythm of the camel's gait, he was reminded that the pure things of God did not need the publicity or drama of the world's pleasures. The steady, quiet, unwavering faith he had learned from Abraham was enough—it brought profound wisdom and patience with it. As he looked across the vast landscape ahead, he reminded himself that he was a man of faith venturing into the unknown, relying not on his strength or wisdom, but on the profound assurance that a higher power would guide his steps. Eliezer was in shock at the peace that swept over him and everyone on this trip.

Eliezer found that this peculiar sense of peace was both humbling and stirring. He felt like he was the humble instrument being played in the hands of a master in the theater he had been in, in Turkey, with Abraham five years ago, when they went there to make a trade deal.

Now, today, they were stopping just short of the Lebanon to their East and the Euphrates River to their Northeast. This rich area would also bring increased threats. The journey through the borderlands presented a different kind of challenge. These were regions where cultures and customs often intermingled, where the familiar gave way to the subtly different. They would have to be constantly observant and cautious.

The land itself began to transform. The sparse scrub of the southern regions gradually yielded to more robust vegetation. Patches of wild herbs, their scents released by the morning dew, perfumed the air with a subtle, earthy fragrance. Eliezer, with his keen senses honed by years of devoted service, absorbed every detail. He noted the changing patterns of the stars at night, the subtle shifts in the wind's direction, and the calls of birds he did not recognize; each observation was a quiet confirmation of his movement away from the known and into the unfolding purpose of his quest.

As he pressed northward, the whispers of the land grew louder, speaking of ancient forests and the cool breath of mountains. The air itself began to carry a different scent, a crisp, resinous aroma that grew stronger with each mile. It was the fragrance of cedar, the noble trees for which this land, Lebanon, was destined to be renowned. Eliezer had heard tales of these cedars, towering sentinels of the earth, whose wood was prized for its strength, fragrance, and enduring quality. He imagined them now, a verdant cloak upon the mountainsides, a stark contrast to the ochre and brown palette of the Judean wilderness. This was a land of abundance, a place where life flourished in the embrace of the mountains.

His journey was not one of haste, but of mindful progression. Eliezer was a man deeply attuned to the nuances of the world around him, and he understood that true understanding came from patient observation and reflection. He saw the small villages nestled in the valleys, smoke curling from their hearths, the sounds of daily life—laughter, the ringing of hammers, the bleating of goats—drifting on the breeze. He observed the people he encountered along the dusty tracks: farmers tending their fields, merchants leading their laden donkeys, women drawing water from ancient wells.

Each interaction, however brief, was an opportunity to gauge the spirit of the land and its inhabitants. He offered greetings, sometimes shared a portion of his provisions, and always carried himself with a quiet dignity that invited respect rather than suspicion. His focus remained unwavering: to find a woman worthy of Isaac, a woman whose inner beauty would complement his gentle soul.

Eliezer was astonished at how his thoughts kept wandering on this trip. It was almost as if Abraham or a historian were riding with him, telling him stories and reminding him of the character of his Master, Abraham, and his son, Isaac.

Finally, Eliezer decided that he needed to gather his thoughts, as Isaac's new bride would likely have many questions about her new home, husband, and father-in-law. Maybe that was why God was letting his thoughts wander. He had to recall what he would need to share with this young lady so that she could be the bride she needed to be—one in love with her husband, even though she had not seen him before!

He pondered Isaac's character, the quiet strength that lay beneath his unassuming exterior. Isaac was not a man of grand pronouncements or bold displays, but of deep kindness, unwavering loyalty, and a profound capacity for love. He possessed a rare serenity, a gentle spirit that seemed to draw others towards him. Eliezer had witnessed this firsthand, seen how Isaac's presence could calm troubled waters, how his words, though few, often carried the weight of wisdom. The woman Eliezer sought must be one who could appreciate these qualities, one who would not be intimidated by Isaac's quietude but would instead find in it a sanctuary. She needed a spirit that resonated with his own, a shared understanding that transcended spoken words.

The ideal companion, Eliezer mused, would possess a heart that mirrored the enduring strength and gentle fragrance of the cedars he was approaching. She would have the resilience to weather life's storms, the grace to nurture growth, and a natural inclination towards kindness. Beauty was, of course, a consideration, for Isaac was a man of refinement. But it was not the superficial allure of outward appearance that Eliezer sought. He was searching for the radiance that emanates from a soul at peace with itself and with its Creator. He sought a woman whose laughter was like the tinkling of clear water over stones, whose compassion flowed as freely, and whose spirit was as steadfast as the ancient mountains.

As the landscape continued its transformation, Eliezer felt a growing sense of anticipation. The foothills became more pronounced, the air cooler and cleaner. The scent of cedar grew more insistent again.

The route he took was not always the most direct, but it offered glimpses into the heart of the land. He skirted the edges of small farming communities, where the rhythms of life were dictated by the sun and the soil. He saw women working alongside men in the fields, their hands calloused but their spirits seemingly unbroken. He observed the interactions between families, the bonds of kinship evident in their shared labor and their communal meals. Eliezer was not merely a traveler; he was a silent observer, a student of humanity, seeking the thread of divine purpose woven through the fabric of everyday existence.

He allowed his camel to graze on the succulent grasses that grew in sheltered hollows, taking the time to rest and to reflect. The vastness of the sky above him, an expanse of uninterrupted blue stretching from horizon to horizon, offered a profound sense of perspective. It was in these moments of quiet solitude, surrounded by the grandeur of nature, that Eliezer felt most connected to the divine presence that guided his every step. He prayed for discernment, asking for the wisdom to recognize the woman who would be the perfect complement to Isaac—a woman who would not only be a wife but also a true partner, a co-heir of the promises. He sought a woman whose heart was open to God's guidance, whose faith was a living, breathing thing, not merely a learned ritual.

The cedars, now visible on the higher slopes, seemed to beckon him forward. Their majestic presence spoke of endurance, of reaching towards the heavens, of providing shelter and strength. Eliezer felt a kinship with these ancient trees. Like them, he was rooted in a profound tradition, reaching towards a divine purpose, and striving to offer a foundation of stability and grace. He knew that the woman he sought would embody these very qualities. She would be a steadfast presence in Isaac's life, a source of comfort and inspiration, and a vital link in the chain of generations to come.

He had passed the Cedars of Lebanon; now, he had to turn and head toward Mesopotamia (present-day Iraq) to reach the land from which Abraham's parents came. He was officially in virgin territory for himself. He had never been past Lebanon. He had only been through Egypt once, with Abraham, over 50 years ago. Eliezer trusted, with every fiber of his being, that the same God who had guided Abraham would guide his steps, leading him to the fulfillment of this noble quest.

The vastness of the landscape unfolded before him, a tapestry of green and blue, where he hoped to find a reflection of the inner beauty he so earnestly sought. He saw the land not just as a destination, but as a testament to God's enduring provision. Eliezer felt the profound significance of his journey, a pilgrimage not just of miles, but of spirit, a quest to unite two souls destined to carry forward a legacy of faith that would bless generations to come.

The road, once a winding ribbon through rolling hills, now opened into broader valleys, and Eliezer found himself drawn towards the faint hum of human activity. He saw them first as distant figures, moving with a purposeful gait, then as closer shapes against the vibrant green of cultivated fields. These were the inhabitants of Iraq. He was closer to the section called Ur.

### Finishing up week three of travel:

He was about to give up on reaching the next village before nightfall when they reached the top of the hill. He was delighted to see a large village nestled in the valley below. There were small clusters of dwellings scattered around the valley as if they were protecting the buildings in the center.

It took them several hours to wind down the mountains and work their way toward the center of this town. The were entering from the southwest side of the village. To his right, he saw a group of women walking with water jugs heading northwest. He assumed that must be the direction of the well. That is the best place to meet the women of this village. However, nightfall would soon arrive, and they desperately needed certain supplies. The well would have to wait till morning.

As he progressed further down this path, Eliezer realized he was entering into a bustling marketplace for a town this size. He was amazed until he remembered that the Euphrates River was nearby. His caravan had entered from the Southwest side of town. On the northeast side of this valley, there was a direct path to the river. It was an open road, no hills, just a straight shot to the river, so the guy at the last village had said. He said this valley was home to some of the wealthiest merchants in Mesopotamia. This village was called Nahor. That name sounds familiar. He was going to have to review the notes he had jotted down on a tablet while Abraham was talking at supper the night before they started this journey. He was so tired that he would not think straight right now.

The souk was filled with makeshift booths and open-air stores selling a variety of food items. There was much noise. Oh, the smell was gagging him. He forgot how bad fish and animals smelled after having five weeks on the open road with clean, fresh air to breathe. Eliezer looked around as the merchants called out their wares to him, trying to get him in their sights. They needed to make one last big sale of the day. The last sale was almost as important as the first sale of the day.

Superstition in these former Medi-Persian countries was that the first sale of the day determined whether or not the gods would have favor on your business that day. They believed that if you were courteous, honest, and gave the first customer of the day your best possible price, then you would have many sales. If, for some reason, you did not close the first sale, then it was going to be a rough day without much success! Even though Eliezer did not believe this—he knew Yahweh was the one who determined blessings and cursing—he loved this concept because he always tried to be the first customer or the last customer of the day. It was just good business sense to take advantage of the markdowns!

He could not help but notice the beautiful merchandise from many different countries as he walked through to the city business center—brightly colored textiles, gleaming pottery, mounds of fragrant spices, and the ubiquitous produce of the fertile land. Eliezer had never seen such a large variety of fresh fruits and vegetables in one market. He recognized hand-made woven rugs of the highest quality from Damascus, silk from Egypt, women's clothes from Greece, perfumes from France, jewelry and pottery from Morocco. He must find time to buy something for his wife before he leaves this place.

Now he was where the horrible scent was coming from—the farm center—the farmers were arguing and haggling over the price of their animals. To the right were the stands selling vegetables and fruits. The people managing these must have made good morning deals and were experiencing the favor of the gods, because their faces were lit with the satisfaction of a good sale. So much different from the furrowed brows across the street, where there were obvious concerns—probably less favorable bargains.

Eliezer noticed that the women in their group had instantly been drawn to several local artisans displays. Their crafts were exquisite. The details were like nothing he had ever seen before. It was apparent that the amount of love and sweat that went into making these items. Immediately, his mind wandered to who the artists were in the crowd around that booth. Why were they so passionate about their labors? What drew people to these products—he was sure the prices were very high.

Finally, he was at the business center. The place where the elders of the town sit in their favorite chairs or on their favorite stools each day, discussing what is happening and making joint decisions about imports and exports. (This group would be equivalent to our tourism office, chamber of commerce, and city council all in one group.)

These men introduced themselves to Eliezer and his two sons. They had left the camels and all of the caravan supplies outside of town at the end of the clearing as they made their way to the end of the mountain pass. He wanted to talk to the people of the city without everyone assuming he was rich or representing a rich man. He did not want their advice improperly influenced.

Once he had the information he needed, he would rejoin the caravan, and they would find the perfect place to camp. This village was more like a town or a city.

He could rent a room for the women here. The main reason he brought them in with him.

## The last night of the fourth week:

Eliezer got the information he needed from the elders. He had been told that this was the village where Abraham and his brother Nahor had once lived and done business. These elders confirmed that info. But that was 78 years ago. So, no one present even remembered what the two looked like--they only recognized the names. They thought that the area Eliezer was looking for was about 150 miles further by road.

## The next morning:

After a good night's sleep and breakfast, Eliezer decided to revisit the town center, get a few more supplies, and then take the camels to the well. This would give him some time to observe the locals and learn more about the customs and gods of the area. He needed all the info possible before he made it to Abraham's brother's house or whoever was still left alive.

By the time he had made his purchases and they had packed everything up to hit the road again, it was mid-morning (around 9 am our time). The early morning group of women had already left the well. The group that was here now was those older women who had more time. They were not in a rush. Eliezer thought, "This is good; maybe I can talk to some of them." Once they are through getting their water, my men and I will water the camels. It had been almost a week since he had watered them thoroughly. They had only had a couple of small waterings because the other villages were so small. Ten camels could require as much as 300 gallons of water in under 30 minutes, drastically lowering the levels in a small well.

The camels that were brought on this trip were Abraham's top ten camels. They were young and energetic. Each time he gave them to drink, he had to draw 300 gallons or more of water to fill them up. They could easily hold 30 gallons of water at a time. They can survive up to two weeks without water in extreme conditions, but that is not ideal for them. Eliezer always tried to make sure that he watered them every five to seven days. More often, if water was available. When traveling for so long, it is best to take advantage of restocking their water supply and filling the camels up at every possible place, so if they ran into a section of desert where they could only get water for themselves and not the camels (due to a small well), the camels would be fine. The heat could be fatal to humans without water.

The women at the well were very friendly and respectful. He exchanged greetings with most of them. He told them that he would water his camels when they were finished. This allowed him to do what he loved most—people watching!

When the women had finished with their task and completed their family chats and interactions, Eliezer's servants moved forward and started watering the camels. The sun was going to be straight up by the time they left this valley. That was later than Eliezer had planned, but where they were going to stay tonight was only nine to ten miles away. So, no rush.

### The fourth week of travel is almost over:

They have reached another village, further north along the Euphrates River. This is a bustling little port city. Amidst this lively exchange, Eliezer was not merely an observer of commerce; he was a student of human nature. He watched the interactions, the subtle gestures, the expressions that revealed the underlying motivations of each individual. He saw generosity in a merchant who offered a small sample of his fruit to a curious child, and he saw a quiet desperation in another who seemed to plead with potential customers. These were the threads of life, interwoven and complex, and Eliezer sought to discern the pattern of true character within them.

He found himself drawn to a stall where an elderly man was meticulously arranging bundles of dried herbs, their distinct fragrances mingling to create an intoxicating aroma. The man's hands, gnarled with age, moved with a surprising nimbleness as he sorted the leaves and flowers.

Eliezer paused, appreciating the care with which the man worked. He engaged the merchant in conversation, inquiring about the properties of the herbs and their uses in both healing and daily life. The older man spoke with a gentle wisdom; his words laced with a deep understanding of the natural world. He spoke of the earth's bounty, of the healing power that resided within even the humblest plant, and of the importance of respecting the gifts that were so freely given.

Eliezer listened, his mind not only absorbing the practical knowledge but also reflecting on the deeper principles the man conveyed. It was a reminder that true value was often found not in grand pronouncements, but in the quiet, consistent offering of service and the nurturing of life. The merchant's dedication to his craft and his reverence for the natural world resonated with Eliezer's purpose. He saw in the man a reflection of the deep-rooted faith and steadfastness he hoped to find in Isaac's future wife.

They made camp outside the village that night. When the sun began to come up, like every other day and week on this trip, all the servants were up and fully engaged in their routines. Everything was working in sync. Eliezer's goal had been to reach a village that the last souk owner he had spoken with the previous day had

50

mentioned. It was a small village nestled in a valley, its houses built of stone, their roofs weathered by time and elements.

As he saw the village approaching in the distance, he thought he smelled the faint scent of freshly baked bread. Surely that was his imagination. The village was too far away. However, as they grew nearer, the smell grew stronger. It was calling to all travelers to stop, rest, and eat.

As they arrived in the village, Eliezer saw children playing in the dusty lanes, their laughter echoing against the ancient walls. He observed families gathered in courtyards, sharing meals and conversation. The man in the last souk had said this was where the women and men of Ur came to buy and sell. He also noted that there were small villages outside this town. One might be the very village I was looking for, or at least would get him closer.

Eliezer found a quiet place to rest his camels near the edge of the village, and they set up camp for the night. After their evening meal, Eliezer and his two sons walked into the town to look around. They watched a father teaching his son how to mend a fishing net, their heads bent close together in shared concentration. He saw a mother comforting a child who had stumbled, her touch gentle, her words soothing. These were the intimate moments that formed the fabric of a family, the quiet acts of love and dedication that built the foundation of a life.

Another day was coming to an end. They had not found Abraham's brothers, but he could feel it in his gut. He was getting close to wherever God was leading him.

The next morning, Eliezer continues his journey, the images and impressions of the day settling within him. The encounters, though brief, were not mere detours; they were integral to his mission. Each conversation, each observation, served as a subtle calibration of his discernment, a gentle nudging towards clarity. He was sifting through the vast spectrum of human experience, seeking that singular thread of character that would complement Isaac's gentle soul. He was looking for a woman whose spirit would be as enduring as the cedar trees that now towered on the mountainsides, a woman whose inner beauty would be as profound and as fragrant as the very essence of this noble land.

The fourth week of travel had been worse than the three preceding it. Not because of the terrain, but because they were not covering as much ground as they thought they would cover per day. There are too many small villages and towns to go through. It slowed a Caravan this size down significantly. Today had been the worst day of the week. It was his fourth week on this journey, and he knew it would never end. He could not stand the thought of staying there for two weeks and then having to make a five-week trip back. At least the return trip would be quicker because he would know where he was going, not having to hunt for directions.

After two more days of traveling (the last day of the fourth week), Eliezer stumbled upon a small, secluded grove of ancient olive trees. Their gnarled trunks, twisted and weathered by centuries, spoke of a deep history, of seasons of plenty and seasons of hardship. Beneath the shade of these venerable trees, a young woman sat, her head bowed over a small basket of fallen olives. She worked with a quiet intensity, her fingers deftly separating the good fruit from the bruised.

Eliezer approached cautiously, not wishing to startle her. As he drew nearer, he saw that her face, though smudged with the earth from her labor, possessed a natural, unadorned beauty. Her eyes, when she looked up at his approach, were clear and thoughtful, holding a depth that belied her youthful appearance. He greeted her with a gentle inclination of his head, and she responded with a shy but warm smile, her gaze direct yet unassuming.

They spoke for a time, Eliezer inquiring about the olive harvest, a staple of the region. She explained the process with quiet knowledge, using clear and precise words. She spoke of the cyclical nature of the harvest, the dependence on the weather, and the shared effort involved. Eliezer listened, noting the way she spoke of her family's involvement, the collective responsibility they shared in tending these ancient trees. There was no pretense in her words, no desire to impress, only a simple recounting of their way of life. He asked about her life in the village, and she spoke of the community's close ties, the shared celebrations, and mutual support. Eliezer observed the genuine affection in her voice when she spoke of her family, as well as the quiet pride in their shared labor.

When he inquired, she admitted that her husband owned that olive grove. She said it would be okay for them to camp there for the night and to have a day of rest the following day. He was so grateful. They all needed the rest, and the animals would appreciate having the grove for shade.

**The fifth week of travel:**

What struck Eliezer as amusing about this final week of travel was how much his mind kept wandering back to the last woman he had spoken with the previous week. What was most profound was her demeanor. There was a serenity about her, something about her demeanor that said, "I am stable, grounded, educated, and mature beyond my years." Her calm, in-control attitude seemed to emanate from her very being. Even in her simple task, there was a grace, a focused intent that spoke of a disciplined spirit. He saw in her hands, which were capable and strong, the evidence of honest work, and in her eyes, the reflection of a contemplative soul. Eliezer considered

53

the qualities he sought in Isaac: a woman of inner strength, unwavering integrity, and a gentle, loving spirit.

He remembered how he conversed with this young woman at the well and then with her and her husband on the day of rest. As his mind compared Isaac and this man, he felt a quiet stirring within him, a sense that he was witnessing a glimpse of what he had been searching for in a wife for Isaac. This man's wife was humble, resilient, and had an eager, faithful spirit. She was not down, depressed, or grumpy. Even when she spoke of sad times or difficulties, she did so in a positive manner. These qualities deeply impressed him. He did not press her with direct questions about marriage or family life, for that would have been too forward.

Instead, he allowed the conversations they had over that two-day period to flow naturally, observing and absorbing. He noted the way she expressed gratitude for the bounty of the land, her simple faith evident in her words. She spoke of the importance of family, not just as a unit of relation, but as a sacred trust, a place of refuge and growth. Eliezer felt a resonance with her perspective, a confirmation of his own beliefs about the foundational importance of a strong, loving union.

Why was his mind wandering so much today? He needed to get focused. They had to decide where to stay for the night and which way to go when they arrived at the area where the locals said three roads met. He anticipated reaching that area the following day. However, each of these encounters, from the women at the well to the merchants in the marketplace, the young woman and her husband in the olive grove, and others along this journey, was more than just a passing interaction. They were moments of profound reflection, each one adding another layer to Eliezer's understanding of the people and the land of the Chaldeans. He saw not just individuals, but reflections of a way of life, a deep connection to tradition, family, and the divine. He was sifting through the many facets of human character, looking for the one that would harmonize perfectly with Isaac's gentle spirit.

## The fourth day of the fifth week since leaving Gaza:

Up at sun break again, rested, energized, and ready to go. He was excited about what the merchant had told him the night before about the next village and the town that passed it. Once they got through this winding trail and took the road (where the three roads meet), they would be turning toward Mesopotamia. Almost there! Then, under his breath, he prayed for God to bless his trip to this well and let this be the day that he was victorious. Somehow, he knew that tomorrow would bring victory. He did not know how to explain this—but he was certain.

There were problems with the sheep and goats. This has been a long trip for them. They are irritable and probably need rest his Shepherd stated. The women also required more stops today. The mileage they planned to cover today was going to take two and a half days. Eliezer kept reminding his sons to stop complaining. God has a plan. He understands what is going on. Maybe the wife of Isaac is with her family in Mesopotamia on a business trip. Perhaps we need an extra day or so for her to get home. We cannot rush God or his will. We must remain patient, and as we wait, we must do it with honor, integrity, and humility.

## Day six of the fifth week—Eliezer meets the perfect woman:

Finally, they have arrived, two and a half days later than planned. Eliezer wanted to arrive at the well for the early morning watering. Tomorrow was the day of rest, and he felt really obligated to give that to God. He did not want to be "wife searching" on the day of rest. He was not happy about the delay, but he felt at peace about it anyway.

Instead of searching for a place to make camp, there was something "dragging" Eliezer to the well. He did not understand this; this had not happened at all on this trip. But something was different about today and about going to the well. Typically, he would have set up camp, bought supplies, and then gone to the well.

He stopped and dismounted from the camel. He walked back to each of the 10 men on camels and gave them instructions to follow him, not to go ahead with setting up camp. They looked at him with strange looks. His two sons asked if he was okay. He informed them, yes, but they had to water the animals first this time.

When they arrived at this well, it was evident that it was the nexus of life in this sun-drenched valley. Somehow, this was more than just a source of water; it was a place where the community's rhythm found its pulse, where stories were exchanged, and where the daily rituals of life unfolded. In this village, the well was the center of business.

As he approached, the gentle murmur of voices reached him, a tapestry of feminine conversation woven with the clinking of pottery and the soft splash of water. He saw women engaged in the age-old task of drawing sustenance from the earth's deep reservoirs, their movements fluid and accustomed. They were the keepers of the hearth, the nurturers of families, and it was here, amidst the very fabric of their lives, that Eliezer felt the weight of his mission settle upon him with renewed intensity.

In the distance, sitting under palm trees with another olive grove close by. Planted as if it were planned to block the noonday and evening sun from where the men would sit and protect the well for the women. This area was beautiful. Its purpose is completely defined.

56

Eliezer dismounted his camel, securing it with a practiced hand, and then, finding a secluded spot a short distance away, on a rise that offered a clear view of the well without intruding upon the women's gathering, he knelt. The air was still, save for the distant chirping of birds and the soft rustling of olive leaves in the gentle breeze. Eliezer bowed his head, his hands pressed together, his heart a conduit for a fervent prayer.

He spoke not in eloquent pronouncements, but in the quiet, earnest language of a soul seeking divine intervention. "Father," he began, his voice a low whisper that seemed to carry on the very breath of the land, "You who have guided my steps across vast distances, who have provided for me and protected me on this sacred quest, I come before You now with a humble and expectant heart."

He paused, allowing the immensity of his supplication to fill the silence. "I seek Your confirmation, Father. The path has been long, and the encounters, though illuminating, have left me with questions that only Your wisdom can answer. I have seen kindness, strength, and devotion in glimpses, but how am I to discern the one You have chosen for Isaac?"

His gaze drifted towards the well, where he observed the serene yet purposeful actions of the women. "Lord," Eliezer continued, his voice tinged with the vulnerability of a father's deep concern, "I ask for a sign, a clear indication that I am on the right path. Not a sign of grandeur, but one of quiet certainty, a whisper of Your will that will banish all doubt and reassure my heart that you indeed bless this undertaking."

He thought of the woman he envisioned for Isaac. Not one who craved the fleeting attention of the world, but one whose inner beauty shone forth like a hidden gem. A woman whose hands, though accustomed to honest labor, were also capable of gentle solace. A woman whose faith was not a mere outward show, but a deep, unwavering anchor in the storms of life. A woman who would find her greatest joy in the simple, enduring commitments of family, in the shared labor of love, and the quiet worship of You. "Father, I pray for discernment. Please grant me the wisdom to recognize these qualities, to see beyond the superficial, and to perceive the true essence of a soul. Protect me from being swayed by outward appearances, by charm that masks a shallow heart, or by strength that hardens into pride."

Eliezer's prayer deepened, touching upon the very core of his hopes and anxieties. He articulated the fears that had sometimes whispered at the edges of his resolve. The fear of choosing wrongly, of leading Isaac down a path that would bring him sorrow instead of fulfillment. The fear that his judgment might be clouded by desire or by a misplaced sense of urgency. "Guide my discernment, Father. Let my eyes see what You wish me to see, and my heart understand what You intend for me to understand. I place Isaac's future into Your loving hands, for I know that Your plan for him is far greater and more perfect than anything I can conceive."

Eliezer continued to pray, "If there is a woman here, Father, whose spirit is aligned with the principles of Abraham and who has a heart like Isaac's, open to your will, and whose character reflects your light, reveal her to me. I am ready to receive Your guidance, to embrace the path You have laid out."

His prayer was not a demand, but an offering. An offering of his trust, his faith, and his unwavering love for Isaac. He remained in that posture of humble supplication, his eyes closed, his mind focused, waiting for confirmation —a subtle nudge from the Divine, a sense of peace that would signify his alignment with God's will. The sun warmed his face, and the sounds of the well, though still present, seemed to recede as he journeyed inward, seeking that profound connection.

He felt a deep sense of peace settle over him, a calm assurance that even amid his questioning, he was not alone. The very act of praying, of surrendering his own will to a higher purpose, was in itself a form of confirmation. It was a testament to his faith, a declaration that he trusted the wisdom of a power far greater than his own.

He opened his eyes, and the scene before him was unchanged, yet subtly different. The women continued their tasks, their movements a familiar dance of daily life. But now, Eliezer saw them with a renewed clarity, his prayer having sharpened his perception. He looked for a particular quality, a certain resonance that had been hinted at in his earlier encounters. He was not seeking perfection, for he knew that such a thing was reserved for the divine. But he was seeking authenticity, a genuine spirit that would be a faithful companion for Isaac's gentle soul. He sought a woman whose inner light would be a beacon, guiding not only her own life but also the life of the man she would choose to share it with.

Eliezer bowed his head again and finished his prayer. He wanted to make sure that Abraham's God understood completely how desperate he was and how sincere he was in asking for a sign to help him make the right choice. He prayed for a woman who understood that true strength lay not in dominance, but in quiet resilience; not in self-assertion, but in steadfast commitment; not in worldly acclaim, but in the profound satisfaction that comes from a life lived by divine principles. He prayed for a woman whose spirit was as deeply rooted as the ancient olive trees, whose character was as enduring as the cedars of Lebanon, and whose love would be as life-giving as the waters drawn from this very well.

Eliezer stayed there for a considerable time, his prayer a silent, continuous stream. He observed the interactions between the women, the subtle exchanges that revealed their inner dispositions. He noted the way one woman patiently helped another with a heavy pail, the gentle laughter shared over a minor mishap, and the quiet empathy displayed when one spoke of a concern. These were the small, unvarnished moments of life, and it was in these moments, Eliezer believed, that true character was most clearly revealed. He was not looking for a grand gesture, but for the consistent thread of kindness, of generosity, of an unpretentious spirit that consistently sought to uplift and support.

He found himself particularly drawn to a woman who was not the loudest in conversation, nor the most demonstrative, but who possessed a quiet grace. She moved with an economy of motion, her actions efficient and purposeful. When she spoke, her voice was soft, yet clear, and her words carried a thoughtful weight. There was a serenity about her that seemed to emanate from a deep inner peace.

Eliezer watched as she helped a younger woman secure a strap on a water skin, her touch gentle, her expression one of quiet encouragement. He saw the way she listened attentively when another spoke, her gaze steady and engaged, reflecting a genuine interest in what was being said. There was no superficiality in her demeanor, no seeking of attention, only a natural, unassuming presence that spoke of a soul at ease with itself and with the world.

He felt a stir within him, a sense of quiet recognition, as if a long-dormant chord had been struck. This was the kind of woman who could be a true partner, a faithful companion. A woman whose strength lay not in outward displays, but in the steadfastness of her spirit, in the depth of her compassion, and the quiet radiance of her inner life. A woman who would, Eliezer felt with a growing certainty, find profound fulfillment in building a life rooted in faith, family, and devotion.

Eliezer continued to pray, asking for clarity, for the final piece of confirmation that would allow him to move forward with confidence. He knew that God's signs were often subtle, requiring a receptive heart and a discerning spirit to perceive them. And in that quiet moment, kneeling by the well, Eliezer felt a profound sense of peace—a calm certainty that he was indeed being led, and that the answer to his fervent prayer was drawing near.

The well, a symbol of life-giving sustenance, had also become a place of spiritual nourishment, a place where his faith was being tested and refined, and where the path forward was beginning to illuminate. He rose, his heart lighter, the weight of uncertainty replaced by a burgeoning hope, and a deep gratitude for the divine guidance that had brought him to this sacred moment. He knew his work was not yet done, but he felt equipped with a renewed sense of purpose, ready to seek out the woman who embodied the quiet virtues he had so earnestly prayed for.

*His heart beat with passion, and his respirations became shallow and fast—he could feel it—the one was here, possibly approaching or already in line. He thought his heart would beat out of his chest!*

"Isaac and Rebekah" by La Wanda Blackmon

# <u>Chapter Four:</u>

# *The Meeting at the Well*

---

It is day six of the fifth week. The midday sun is baking down on Eliezer and his companions with vengeance. He is about 100 yards away from the cement half-wall (made from rocks of all sizes and some mortar) that surrounds the area where the well is.

As he approaches with his camels, he notices that the wall is lined halfway around with women waiting for their turn at the well. With a puzzled look on his face, he is wondering why there are so many people here today at this time. He thought the morning rush would have been over at least three hours ago. However, Eliezer was drawn to this group like a magnet. He could not take his eyes away from their line of waiters. There was that rapid heartbeat again. What was going on with him? Why was Yahweh doing this to him? Unless it meant that the one was here!

The well itself was a focal point, a circular aperture carved into the earth, its rough-hewn edges worn smooth by countless hands over uncounted generations. Around it, a tableau of daily life unfolded with a gentle, unhurried rhythm. The air thrummed with a low hum of conversation, a tapestry of feminine voices, some lilting and melodious, others more profound and more resonant, all woven together with the percussive symphony of pottery clinking against stone and the soft, rhythmic splash of water being drawn. It was a scene of profound normalcy, yet for Eliezer, it carried an extraordinary significance. His prayer had been offered, his heart laid bare, and now, he was attuned to every subtle nuance, every fleeting expression, waiting for the whisper of divine confirmation.

He had watched as women, their movements practiced and economical, filled their vessels, their faces shaded by the simple coverings that afforded protection from the sun. There was a strength in their bearing, a quiet dignity in their labor, that resonated deeply with the qualities he had sought for Isaac. They were not adorned with the superficial trappings of wealth or status, but possessed a more profound richness—the richness of a life lived in purpose, of hands capable of both honest toil and gentle care. Eliezer felt a growing sense of anticipation, a quiet stirring within his soul, as if the very air around him was vibrating with an unseen energy, a prelude to the revelation he so earnestly sought.

And then, his attention was arrested. Amidst the familiar flow of activity, a new figure emerged from the periphery, drawing his gaze with an arresting grace. It was a young woman, her steps measured and unhurried as she approached the well. She carried no vessel, her hands clasped loosely before her, as if she had come to observe or perhaps to offer assistance. Eliezer noted the way she moved, not with the hurried urgency of someone burdened by the heat or the labor, but with a serene composure that seemed to set her apart. Her head was slightly bowed, her gaze directed towards the well, a posture that conveyed a sense of humility and respect for the communal space.

As she drew nearer, Eliezer could discern more of her features, softened by the distance and the oblique angle of the sun. Her face, though partially shadowed, seemed to possess a natural beauty, unmarked by the artifice of adornment. It was the kind of beauty that spoke of an inner radiance, a quiet strength that emanated from within. He observed her interaction with the other women; she offered a quiet word to one, a gentle smile to another, her presence a subtle balm to the bustling atmosphere. There was no boastfulness in her manner, no seeking of attention, only a genuine, unassuming warmth. It was in these small, unstudied gestures that Eliezer began to perceive the qualities he had so fervently prayed for.

He watched as an older woman, her arms laden with two heavy clay jars, stumbled slightly, her grip faltering. Before Eliezer could even fully register the near mishap, the young woman was there, her hand reaching out with an almost imperceptible swiftness, steadying the jars and offering a quiet, reassuring word. There was no fuss, no grand display of helpfulness, just an instinctive act of kindness, a seamless integration into the fabric of communal support. Eliezer felt a surge of affirmation, a quiet resonance within his spirit. This was not a rehearsed performance; this was the natural outflow of a compassionate heart.

The setting itself seemed to conspire in this unfolding revelation. The ancient stones of the well, warmed by the sun, offered a tactile testament to the enduring nature of this place, a place where generations had drawn not only water but also sustenance for their lives and their souls. The air, thick with the scent of dust and the faint, sweet perfume of distant wildflowers, seemed to hold its breath, as if acknowledging the sacredness of the moment. The murmurs of the other women, the rhythmic dipping of buckets, and the calls of children playing nearby all contributed to a rich auditory landscape that Eliezer absorbed with heightened sensitivity. He was not merely observing; he was receiving, his senses attuned to the subtle language of truth.

Eliezer had envisioned a woman whose strength was not a brittle facade, but a deep, resilient core; a woman whose faith was not a mere outward profession, but an intrinsic part of her being. Yet at the same time, he was wondering how he would find all of this in a young lady between the ages of 12 and 16. The age of 14 was the best time to select a wife. She would be young and fresh, not yet contaminated by the world or its idols.

The young woman that Eliezer was looking at appeared to be between 14 and 16 years of age. But she had the wisdom and heart of a 25-year-old. She did not miss anything that was happening around her, nor did she pass up a chance to help someone. She had no idea that she was being watched today, as if she were auditioning for a job or an award. She was working hard today, maintaining her quiet composure and an unassuming demeanor as she went about her work. As he watched, Eliezer could feel his heartstrings confirming for him that this was the one!

He continued to watch, his gaze unwavering, as she moved among the women. He saw the way she listened, truly listened, when another spoke; her expression was open and engaged, reflecting genuine interest and empathy. There was a depth in her eyes, a quiet intelligence that hinted at a mind that was both keen and contemplative. She did not dominate the conversation, but when she spoke, her words were thoughtful, measured, and carried a gentle wisdom. It was as if her very presence brought a sense of calm to the bustling activity, a quiet anchoring amid the day's demands.

Eliezer found himself comparing her to the women he had encountered previously on his journey. There had been those who were boisterous and attention-seeking, their words filled with a superficial charm that masked a hollowness. There had been others whose outward piety seemed a mere performance, lacking the genuine substance of actual devotion. But this young woman—she was different. Her virtues were not flaunted; they were lived. They were woven into the very fabric of her being, evident in the quiet integrity of her demeanor, in the unpretentious kindness of her actions.

He prayed that if this were indeed the woman God had chosen for Isaac, her heart would be fertile ground, receptive to the seeds of love and commitment that Isaac would plant. He prayed that her spirit would be strong enough to weather the inevitable storms of life, yet gentle enough to nurture the delicate blooms of a shared future. He prayed that her devotion to God would be the bedrock of her life, guiding her actions and shaping her character, so that she would be a true reflection of the divine love he envisioned.

The sun climbed higher, its intensity increasing, yet Eliezer remained, his focus unwavering. He was not seeking a dramatic sign, no thunderclap or celestial manifestation. He was seeking the quiet certainty that resonated with the profound truths he held dear. He was looking for the silent confirmation that would whisper to his soul, a confirmation that this was the path, this was the woman, divinely appointed for Isaac's future.

And in the serene grace, the unassuming kindness, and the quiet strength of the young woman before him, Eliezer felt that whisper beginning to form, a nascent assurance that the wellspring of providence was indeed beginning to reveal its precious bounty. The rhythmic splash of water, the murmuring voices, and the warmth of the sun—all coalesced into a moment of profound clarity, a moment where faith and anticipation converged, and the journey toward a divinely ordained union felt palpably closer.

He saw her turn, her gaze briefly sweeping over the landscape, and for a fleeting instant, Eliezer felt as though her eyes might have met his, a silent acknowledgment across the sun-drenched space. It was a moment so brief, so ethereal, that he could not be certain, but it added another layer to the growing conviction in his heart. He knew that the next steps would require discernment and prudence. Still, for now, he absorbed the essence of this vision by the water's edge, a vision that felt like the dawning of a new hope, a testament to the enduring power of prayer and the subtle, profound ways in which divine guidance can manifest.

Eliezer observed her as she accepted a small clay jug from another woman, her fingers closing around it with a familiar, competent grip. She then turned and began to walk away from the well, her movements graceful, her silhouette sharp against the shimmering heat waves. Eliezer watched until she was a distant figure, her presence lingering in his mind's eye. The vision, though fleeting, had planted a seed of profound certainty within him. He felt a quiet gratitude for the opportunity to witness such unadorned virtue, a virtue that spoke volumes without the need for grand pronouncements.

The air around him still buzzed with the sounds of the well, but Eliezer's inner world had been transformed. He felt a sense of peace, a quiet joy that emanated from the knowledge that his prayers were being heard and answered, not with the fanfare of trumpets, but with the gentle unveiling of truth, like water seeping from a hidden spring. He stood, his legs stiff from kneeling, and began to descend the rise, his purpose sharpened, his heart filled with a burgeoning hope. The path to a divinely chosen bride for Isaac had begun, and it started here, by this ancient well, under the watchful eye of the midday sun.

Eliezer, concealed yet keenly observant, watched as the woman he had glimpsed earlier moved with a quiet grace towards the edge of the gathering. She wasn't carrying a water vessel, which initially piqued his curiosity further. Her hands were clasped loosely in front of her, not in idleness, but with a poise that suggested a purpose beyond the immediate task of quenching thirst. As she approached the well, a subtle shift in the atmosphere around her occurred. It wasn't a dramatic disruption, but rather a gentle recalibration, as if the collective hum of activity softened in deference to her presence. He noted the unhurried cadence of her steps, a stark contrast to the palpable weariness he'd observed in some of the other women who had already drawn their water. There was a serene composure about her, an inner stillness that seemed to radiate outwards, touching those nearby with its calming influence.

His eyes followed her as she reached the well's edge. She didn't immediately go for a rope or a bucket. Instead, she paused, her gaze sweeping over the scene with a quiet attentiveness. He saw her offer a soft-spoken word to a woman struggling with a weighty jar, her gesture a slight, almost imperceptible movement of support.

Then, she turned her attention towards the animals gathered at the side—the weary, dust-caked camels, their large, liquid eyes conveying a deep, silent thirst. It was then that Eliezer, his heart pounding with a mixture of anticipation and a nascent hope, decided to reveal himself, albeit in a manner that would not betray his true purpose. He rose from his concealed position on the rise, his movements slow and deliberate, and began to make his way down towards the well, his camel patiently awaiting his return. He approached with the demeanor of a weary traveler, his thirst a tangible reality, and his gaze fixed upon the young woman who had so profoundly captured his attention.

As Eliezer drew closer, he made a deliberate effort to appear as just another traveler seeking respite and refreshment. He carried the guise of a man who had journeyed far, his robes bearing the dust of distant lands, his face etched with the lines of sun and wind. He kept his head slightly bowed, a gesture of humility appropriate for a stranger seeking hospitality.

Eliezer saw the young woman turn as he approached, her eyes meeting his for a fleeting moment. There was no suspicion in her gaze, no trace of guardedness, only a gentle curiosity, a quiet acknowledgment of his presence. He saw the intrinsic beauty of her countenance, not in the superficial sense of adornment, but in the pure, unblemished expression of her spirit. Her features were finely chiseled, her eyes large and expressive, reflecting a depth of character that he found immediately compelling. It was the kind of beauty that resonated with a timeless grace, a testament to a life lived with purpose and inner fortitude.

He stopped at a respectful distance from the well, his voice, though tinged with weariness, carrying a clear and courteous tone. "Please," he began, his gaze settling on her, "would you allow me a drink from your well?" He gestured vaguely towards the well, implying that he was a stranger without the means or knowledge to draw water himself. He watched her reaction closely, his soul attuned to the subtle nuances of her response. He was not merely seeking water; he was seeking a confirmation, a sign. And in the way she responded, her composure unwavering, he began to feel that confirmation taking root.

Her reply was immediate and delivered with a natural kindness that seemed to flow from her as effortlessly as water from a spring. "Of course," she said, her voice soft yet clear, carrying easily across the murmur of the other women. She did not hesitate. She did not make him feel as though he was imposing on her. Instead, she moved with a gentle urgency, her actions guided by an innate sense of hospitality. Eliezer observed as she turned back to the well, her hands reaching for the rope with a practiced ease. He noted the strength in her slender arms, the efficiency of her movements as she lowered the bucket into the incredible depths. It was not a struggle; it was a familiar, well-executed task.

As the bucket descended, Eliezer felt a swell of gratitude, a quiet affirmation that his prayers were indeed being heard. He watched as she worked, her focus entirely on the task at hand. She pulled the rope with a steady rhythm, her body conveying a balanced strength, a testament to a life of honest labor. The water that emerged was clear and pure, reflecting the bright midday sky. She filled a small clay cup, the water still cool and glistening on its surface. She extended it towards him, her eyes meeting his once more, a faint, welcoming smile gracing her lips.

"Here, drink," she offered, her gesture simple and unadorned. Eliezer accepted the cup, his fingers brushing lightly against hers. He felt a jolt, a subtle warmth that seemed to transcend the mere physical contact. He drank deeply, the water quenching a thirst that was more than just physical. It was a thirst for confirmation, for a glimpse of the divine in the everyday. As he drank, he continued to observe her. He saw her attention shift again, this time towards his camel, a magnificent creature that stood patiently nearby, its sides heaving slightly from the journey. He noticed the way her gaze lingered on the animal, a silent acknowledgment of its part in his travel.

It was then that she spoke again, her words echoing with a generosity that went beyond the expected courtesies. "And for your camels," she said, her eyes scanning the animal with a thoughtful expression, "I will draw water for them as well." Eliezer felt a profound stillness settle over him. This was more than mere politeness; it was an act of expansive kindness, a willingness to extend help beyond what was directly asked. He had requested water for himself, a simple, immediate need. But she, with an intuitive understanding, had recognized the needs of his companion, the faithful animal that had borne him across the distances.

He watched, his heart swelling with a quiet joy, as she turned back to the well. This time, she began the process of lowering the bucket again, her movements just as efficient and graceful as before. He saw her deftly maneuver the rope, her focus undiminished. The effort involved in drawing water for a single person was significant; drawing water for a string of camels, animals known for their immense thirst, was a considerable undertaking. Yet, she approached it with an unassuming willingness, her spirit unburdened by the extra labor.

He observed the other women at the well. Some glanced towards her, perhaps with a flicker of surprise at her willingness to help a stranger with his animals, but there was no judgment, no envy. Their tasks demanded their full attention, and her act of kindness was absorbed into the ongoing tapestry of communal life. Eliezer, however, saw it for what it truly was: a revelation. It was a clear manifestation of the qualities he had prayed for – a heart that was not only kind but also deeply compassionate, a spirit that instinctively extended itself to alleviate the burdens of others, be they human or animal.

He continued to watch as she drew water for the camels, filling the large troughs that were provided for the animals. Her brow was furrowed slightly in concentration, her muscles taut with the exertion, but her expression remained serene. There was no hint of complaint, no grudging effort. Her generosity was not a calculated act, designed to impress or to earn favor. It was a genuine outflow of a beautiful soul, a testament to the depth of her character. Eliezer found himself comparing her to the superficial gestures he had sometimes encountered on his travels, the outward displays of piety that often masked an inner emptiness. This woman's kindness was different. It was quiet, consistent, and utterly unpretentious.

He realized that a higher purpose had guided his journey, and in this moment, by this well, he was witnessing the fruits of that guidance. The young woman's willingness to draw water for his camels was not merely a hospitable gesture; it was a profound demonstration of a selfless spirit, a willingness to go above and beyond, to embrace a need that was not her own. It was a silent language of the heart, a testament to a character that was both strong and tender, capable of deep empathy and unwavering commitment.

As she finished drawing water for the last camel, she turned back to Eliezer, a faint sheen of perspiration on her brow, her cheeks flushed from the effort. She didn't seek his praise, didn't wait for his effusive thanks. Her satisfaction seemed to stem from the act itself, from the fulfillment of a compassionate impulse. Eliezer, still holding the empty cup, felt a surge of emotion. He knew, with a certainty that resonated deep within his soul, that this was the woman. This was the one whose character, whose intrinsic goodness, would be a perfect complement to Isaac's gentle nature.

He offered his sincere thanks; his voice filled with genuine emotion. "I am deeply grateful," he said, meeting her gaze. "Your kindness is a rare and precious gift." He saw her offer a small, almost shy smile in response. There was no vanity in her acceptance of his gratitude, only a quiet acknowledgement of a shared moment. He continued to observe her as she tidied the area around the well, her movements economical and purposeful. She then turned and began to walk away, her presence still radiating that same calm aura.

Eliezer watched her go, and his heart filled with a profound sense of peace and anticipation. His journey had brought him to this well, and by this well, he had found the answer to his earnest prayers. The wellspring of providence had indeed revealed its bounty, and it was in the form of a young woman whose generosity flowed as freely and as purely as the water she had so selflessly drawn. He knew that this was but the beginning of a sacred undertaking, and that the path ahead would require wisdom and careful discernment.

But for now, he was content to absorb the profound impact of witnessing such unvarnished virtue, a virtue that promised a future of love and devotion. This future felt, in that sun-drenched moment, divinely assured. The image of her selfless act, of her drawing water for his weary camels, was etched into his memory, a testament to the accurate measure of a woman's worth. This worth lay not in outward show, but in the quiet, unwavering generosity of her spirit. He saw her bend to retrieve a small piece of cloth dropped by another woman, her movements fluid and unhurried.

This seemingly minor action, this instinct to restore order and offer a small kindness even as she departed, further solidified the impression of her character. It was a testament to an ingrained habit of thoughtfulness, a constant state of consideration for others that permeated her every action. Eliezer remained by the well for a few moments longer, allowing the magnitude of what he had witnessed to settle within him fully. The sounds of the well, the murmuring voices, the splash of water, all seemed to recede, replaced by the resonant echo of her kindness. He knew that the next steps would involve approaching her family, engaging in the proper customs, and seeking their consent, but the foundation had been laid.

A foundation of profound respect and admiration for a woman whose actions spoke louder than any eloquent declaration. He turned then, his camel nudging him gently, a reminder of his journey. But his steps were lighter, his heart filled with a nascent joy, a quiet certainty that he had indeed found the woman chosen by God for Isaac. The path to this well had been long and arduous, but the reward, he knew, was immeasurable. He had seen a glimpse of a future illuminated by love, guided by faith, and nurtured by a generosity that mirrored the very abundance of God's providence.

The sheer physicality of her labor, as she now turned her attention to his string of ten camels, was a testament to a strength he had only glimpsed earlier. Each camel was a monument of endurance, a creature accustomed to vast distances and arduous treks, and their thirst was correspondingly immense. Eliezer watched, a profound stillness enveloping him, as she expertly maneuvered the rope, her slender arms working with a steady, unwavering rhythm. The bucket, heavy with water, rose from the well's cool embrace, and she poured it into the trough, then repeated the process, and again, and again. It was not a task for the faint of heart, nor for one easily discouraged by exertion. Yet, there was no faltering in her movements, no sigh of weariness that escaped her lips.

He observed the subtle tightening of her muscles, the way her back arched slightly with each pull of the rope, the occasional sheen of perspiration that bloomed on her brow. These were not signs of complaint, but instead natural indicators of honest and dedicated effort. Her focus remained solely on the task, her movements economical and purposeful. It was a quiet diligence, an unpretentious commitment to seeing a need met fully, even when that need extended far beyond the initial request. Eliezer found himself breathing a little easier, the tension that had resided within him for so long beginning to dissipate like mist under the morning sun. This was more than just hospitality; it was a profound demonstration of a generous spirit, a heart that understood the interconnectedness of all life, from the traveler to the faithful beast that bore him.

The wellspring of providence, as he had prayed, was indeed abundant. It flowed not just in the cool, life-sustaining water, but in the character of the one drawing it. He had sought a woman of virtue, a companion whose inner light would guide and sustain Isaac. And here, by this dusty well, under the vast expanse of the sky, he was witnessing a living testament to that prayer. The quiet satisfaction that settled over him was deep and resonant, a melody of faith confirmed. Abraham's trust, placed so firmly in his discernment, was not misplaced. He felt the echoes of his patriarch's faith within him, a shared understanding of the divine orchestration at play. This woman, he knew with a certainty that transcended mere logical deduction, was the answer.

He watched as she continued her work, the rhythmic splash of water against stone, the soft snorts of the camels as they drank, all weaving a comforting symphony. He noticed the way she instinctively adjusted a stray rope, the way her gaze momentarily lingered on a particularly dusty camel, as if to reassure it with her presence. These were the small, almost imperceptible actions that spoke volumes, revealing a depth of empathy that was as vast as the desert he had traversed. It was a kindness that was not performative, not seeking recognition or reward. It was simply an inherent part of her being, as natural and as essential as the air she breathed.

As she finally drew the last bucket of water for the camels, and the animals lowered their heads to drink their fill, she turned back towards Eliezer. The exertion was evident, as was the flush on her cheeks and the slight dampness of her hair clinging to her temples, but her eyes held a quiet, luminous peace. She did not offer a word of complaint, nor did she seek his effusive thanks. Her satisfaction seemed to be derived from the act itself, from the fulfillment of a compassionate impulse. It was a purity of motive that struck Eliezer to his core, a stark contrast to the often-calculating motivations he had encountered in his worldly dealings.

He felt a profound sense of gratitude welling up within him, a silent acknowledgment of the immense effort she had undertaken on his behalf. He had asked for water for himself, a simple request, a traveler's plea. But she, in her innate goodness, had recognized the needs of his entire entourage, extending her generosity to the animals that had so faithfully carried him. This expansive kindness, this willingness to go above and beyond, was the very essence of the character he had prayed for. It was a strength born not of brute force, but of a deeply rooted compassion, a spirit that instinctively sought to alleviate the burdens of others.

He watched as she tidied the area around the well, her movements still imbued with that same quiet efficiency. It was as if the very act of drawing water had become a sacred ritual, performed with grace and purpose. He felt a profound sense of rightness, a deep conviction that his journey had been divinely guided to this very spot, to this same woman. The intricate tapestry of providence was revealing itself in its most beautiful and humble forms, and he was privileged to witness it. He knew that the path ahead would involve the delicate dance of engaging her family, of navigating the customs and traditions that would bind their lives together. But the foundation had been laid, not in elaborate promises or grand pronouncements, but in the simple, profound act of drawing water for a stranger and his camels.

Eliezer remained by the well for a few moments longer, allowing the immense significance of what he had witnessed to settle within him fully. The cacophony of the well, the murmuring voices, the splash of water, all seemed to recede, replaced by the resonant echo of her kindness. He could almost feel the wisdom of Abraham within him, the quiet affirmation that this was indeed the one. He had been sent to find a bride for Isaac, a task that had seemed daunting at first, fraught with the uncertainties of long journeys and the complexities of human hearts. But in this moment, by this well, the answer was clear, radiant, and deeply reassuring.

He knew that the next steps would require careful discernment and adherence to tradition, but the most crucial element—the very heart of the matter—had been revealed. He had found not just a capable woman, but a woman of extraordinary virtue, a woman whose spirit was as pure and as giving as the water she had so selflessly drawn. The path to this well had been long, the journey arduous, but the reward, he knew with an unshakeable certainty, was immeasurable. He had seen a glimpse of a future illuminated by love, guided by faith, and nurtured by a generosity that mirrored the very abundance of God's providence.

The assurance that settled within him was profound, a quiet joy that promised a future of love, devotion, and a partnership built on the bedrock of true character. He felt a deep sense of contentment, a peaceful certainty that the divine plan was unfolding exactly as it was meant to. He offered a silent prayer of thanksgiving, his heart overflowing with gratitude for the profound gift he had been shown.

He watched her finish her task, her movements economical and imbued with a quiet grace that spoke of a life lived in purposeful service. The final bucket lowered, the camels gathered around the trough, their long, elegant necks dipping to quench their thirst. Eliezer felt a profound sense of peace settle over him, a quiet affirmation of his faith and the wisdom of his journey. He had come seeking a bride for Issac who would be a faithful companion, but he realized he had just found more.

This woman, if she would accept his offer, would bring light to Isaac's life and an elite, almost regal demeanor to the rooms she would occupy. He felt she was capable. He whispered a prayer to God, "Please let her be willing to accept this unusual arrangement of marriage. Help her God to adjust to the changes she will have to make. She will have to be willing to accept you as well. So, God, I trust you to check her heart. Then let me know if she is the one."

Eliezer could not believe that he had found such an extraordinary woman with high morals and virtue—it was so evident in how she carried herself. But he realized that he had found a woman of unwavering strength, selfless compassion, inherent dignity, and was more eloquent than he could find words to describe. He had witnessed firsthand the very qualities he had prayed for, qualities that were as vital and life-giving as the water she had so diligently drawn.

As the last of the camels drank their fill and began to amble away, their thirst appeased, she turned back towards him. There was no hint of exhaustion in her demeanor, only a quiet satisfaction, a gentle luminescence in her eyes that seemed to reflect the vast, cerulean sky above. Her gaze met his, not with a demanding expectation of praise, but with a soft, open curiosity. It was in that shared moment, beneath the benevolent gaze of the heavens, that Eliezer knew he must begin to reveal the purpose of his presence. He took a hesitant step forward, his heart resonating with the weight of his mission and the immense privilege of having found such a remarkable soul.

"Forgive my silence thus far," Eliezer began, his voice a low, resonant timbre, carefully modulated to convey respect and sincerity. He paused, allowing his words to settle in the quiet air, observing the subtle shift in her expression, the faint blush that colored her cheeks, a testament to the exertion and perhaps a touch of shyness. "I have been... deeply impressed by your kindness. Not just the hospitality extended to a weary traveler, but the boundless generosity shown to my beasts, ensuring their comfort and well-being. It is a rare quality, a true testament to a noble spirit."

He watched her, noting the way she listened with an attentive stillness, her head tilted slightly, her eyes—the color of warm earth after a spring rain—fixed on his. There was a thoughtful grace in her posture, an unhurried poise that spoke of a deep inner calm. He sensed her gentle nature, the inherent goodness that radiated from her like a gentle warmth. He felt a surge of gratitude, a silent acknowledgment of the immense task that lay before him – to articulate the gravity of his quest and to ascertain if her heart was open to the path he was about to lay before her.

"My journey has been a long one," he continued, choosing his words with deliberate care, "undertaken with a singular purpose. I am not merely a wanderer seeking refreshment, but a messenger, sent by my master, Abraham. He is a man of great faith, a man who has placed his trust in the divine, and who has been blessed accordingly. He sent me forth with a solemn charge, a quest of profound importance." Eliezer took a breath, his gaze steady, seeking to convey the weight of his words without overwhelming her. "He has commanded me to find a wife for his son, Isaac. A son whom he cherishes above all else, a son whose future, and indeed the future of his lineage, rests upon this union."

He observed her reaction closely. Her initial surprise was palpable, evident in the slight widening of her eyes and the soft intake of her breath. Yet, there was no alarm, no immediate withdrawal. Instead, a thoughtful consideration settled upon her features, a quiet contemplation that Eliezer found deeply encouraging. It was as if the very mention of a sacred duty, a divine mandate, resonated with a part of her being.

"My master, Abraham," Eliezer explained, his voice softening as he spoke of his revered employer, "is a man who understands the intricate workings of providence. He believes, with an unshakeable conviction, that the Lord guides our steps, that He orchestrates the paths we take. It was with this profound faith that he sent me, with a prayer on his lips and a clear vision in his heart." He gestured slightly, encompassing the well, the camels, and the woman before him. "He prayed for a sign, a confirmation. He prayed for a woman whose kindness would be evident, whose spirit would be generous, whose hospitality would extend not only to the traveler but also to the creatures that sustained him. He prayed for a woman who would embody the virtues he holds dear, a woman who would bring light and love into Isaac's life."

Eliezer reached into the satchel at his side; his movements deliberate and unhurried. He withdrew two exquisite pieces of jewelry, their surfaces gleaming softly in the dappled sunlight. The first was a delicate pair of gold earrings, intricately crafted, their design reflecting the skilled artistry of the region. The second was a set of elegant gold bracelets, their weight and polish speaking of actual value and precious material. He held them out to her, their gleam a testament to the respect and honor he wished to convey.

"These," he said, offering the gifts with a gentle hand, "are tokens from my master. They are a symbol of his esteem, a preliminary offering of goodwill, and a promise of the future he envisions. Please, accept them as a sign of his sincere regard and the importance he places upon your hospitality and, perhaps, upon your very presence here today." He watched as she hesitated, her gaze flickering from the glittering gold to his face, a mixture of modesty and quiet wonder evident in her expression.

"I... I do not understand," she murmured, her voice barely above a whisper, her hands hovering uncertainly over the offered gifts. "Why would your master send such... such precious things for me?"

Eliezer smiled, a warm, reassuring expression that reached his eyes. "Because, my dear young woman," he said, his voice filled with a gentle earnestness, "the Lord's blessings are often revealed in the simplest of acts, and yet they carry the weight of eternity. Your kindness today was not a simple act; it was a profound demonstration of character, a living embodiment of the qualities my master prayed for. He sent me to find a woman whose heart was as abundant as the wellspring of providence itself, and in you, I believe, I have found her."

He gently placed the earrings and bracelets into her outstretched hands. The cool metal felt substantial against her skin, a tangible sign of the earnestness of his words. She looked down at the gifts, her fingers tracing the delicate patterns of the gold, her mind wrestling with the magnitude of the situation.

"My master's son, Isaac," Eliezer continued, choosing to elaborate further on the man she might one day know, "is a man of quiet strength and deep devotion. He has grown up under the loving guidance of Abraham, a man who has learned, through trials and blessings, the true meaning of faith and integrity. Isaac himself carries these same values, a gentle spirit tempered by a strong will. Abraham desires for him a partner who will share his life, his joys, and his burdens, a companion who will walk with him in faith and love."

82

He paused, allowing the image of Isaac to form in her mind, a man of virtue, destined for greatness, seeking a partner of equal caliber. "A deep certainty guided the journey to this place, a conviction that the Lord would lead me to the one destined for my master's son. And as I observed you, your strength in labor, your compassion for all creatures, and the quiet dignity with which you carry yourself, that certainty only deepened. You have drawn water for my camels, yes, but you have also, in a far more profound sense, drawn forth the answer to a lifelong prayer for my master."

Eliezer continued to speak, detailing the lineage of Abraham, the blessings bestowed upon him, and the enduring covenant that had been established between them. He spoke of the wealth and standing of Abraham's household, not to impress, but to convey the seriousness and the respect with which this union was being considered. He explained the customs and traditions of his people, the importance of family, and the sacred bond of marriage. He painted a picture of a life filled with purpose, love, and a deep connection to the divine.

"Abraham is a man of his word," Eliezer assured her, his voice resonating with the sincerity of his conviction. "He is known for his integrity, his fairness, and his profound faith. He would never offer such a proposal lightly. He has entrusted me with this sacred duty, and I have witnessed firsthand the truth of his discernment. Your character, your spirit, your evident kindness – these are the true treasures, far more valuable than the gold I have presented. These are the qualities that Abraham seeks for his beloved son, qualities that will build a strong and enduring union."

He looked at her, his gaze filled with an earnest hope. "My question, then, is simple, yet it carries the weight of a future yet unwritten. Are you open to this possibility? Are you willing to consider a union with Isaac, the son of Abraham? Are you prepared to journey towards a life that, I believe with all my heart, is divinely ordained for you?"

The silence that followed was charged with unspoken emotions. Rebekah, holding the gifts of gold, her eyes reflecting a myriad of thoughts, appeared to be weighing not just Eliezer's words, but the very implications of his presence and his mission. The encounter at the well, which had begun as a simple act of hospitality, had transformed into a pivotal moment, a crossroads where destiny was beginning to reveal its intricate design. Eliezer waited, his own heart filled with a quiet anticipation, trusting in the providence that had guided him this far. He knew that the answer, whatever it might be, would be delivered with the same gentle honesty that had characterized her every action. The wellspring of providence, indeed, was revealing its depths, and he was privileged to witness its quiet, yet powerful, flow.

The journey from the well to this young woman's family dwelling was a quiet one, yet it resonated with a thousand unspoken thoughts within Rebekah. Eliezer, his stride unhurried and his presence radiating a gentle authority, walked beside her, occasionally glancing at her with an expression of profound respect. She clutched the gold earrings and bracelets in her hands, their weight a tangible reminder of the extraordinary encounter. The well, which had always been a place of daily routine, of selfless service, had suddenly transformed into the stage for a destiny she could scarcely comprehend. Her heart, still fluttering from the enormity of Eliezer's words, was a canvas upon which the first strokes of a grand design were being painted. She felt a curious blend of apprehension and a deep, stirring hope, a sense that the prayers offered by a man she had never met were now intertwining with the very fabric of her own life.

As they approached her family's homestead, the familiar sights and sounds of her home seemed both comforting and strangely distant. The sturdy walls of their dwelling, built to withstand the elements, now felt like the boundaries of a life that was about to expand in ways she could not yet fathom. She could see her father, Bethuel, conversing with her brother, Laban, near the entrance. Laban, ever watchful and eager for opportunity, straightened as they drew closer, his eyes immediately drawn to Eliezer and the unusual aura of importance that seemed to surround him. Bethuel, his face weathered by years of sun and responsibility, turned with a mild curiosity that quickly deepened into surprise as he recognized the stranger who had been at the well.

Rebekah felt a nervous tremor ripple through her as Eliezer began to speak, his voice carrying the same calm assurance that had captivated her by the well. He recounted his journey, his purpose, and the divine guidance he believed had led him to their doorstep. Eliezer spoke of Abraham, his master, a man renowned for his faith and his blessings, a man who sought a wife for his beloved son, Isaac. He presented the gifts again, holding them out to Bethuel and Laban, explaining their significance as tokens of respect and a promise of a profound connection.

The effect of his words and the glittering gold was immediate and electrifying. Laban's eyes widened, not just with surprise, but with an almost palpable avarice. The sheer value of the jewelry was undeniable, a stark contrast to the simple, yet abundant, life they led. He stepped forward, his gaze fixed on the precious metal, his mind already calculating the advantages this union might bring. Wealth, status, a connection to a man of Abraham's stature – these were not merely opportunities; they were visions of a future far grander than anything he had previously imagined.

Bethuel, while perhaps less immediately captivated by the material wealth, was equally struck by the gravity of Eliezer's pronouncement. He understood the significance of lineage, of covenants, and of the divine favor that seemed to rest upon Abraham's house. He listened intently, his brow furrowed in contemplation, his weathered hands resting on his knees. He saw the potential for a powerful alliance, a strengthening of their family's position through such a prestigious connection. The tale Eliezer wove was one of destiny, of a meticulous divine plan that had culminated in this very meeting.

"A wife for Isaac, son of Abraham?" Bethuel echoed, his voice a low rumble, his eyes scanning Eliezer's face for any hint of embellishment or deceit. "You speak of a great man, a man favored by the Most High, Yahweh. And you say he seeks a daughter from our humble dwelling?"

Laban, however, could not contain his enthusiasm. "Precious earrings and bracelets," he exclaimed, his voice laced with awe and excitement as he carefully examined the gifts. "These are not trinkets, esteemed traveler. They speak of a household of great prosperity. To have such a connection... to have Abraham's son take a wife from amongst us..." He trailed off, lost in the glittering possibilities. "Father, this is a remarkable opportunity! A blessing beyond measure!"

Eliezer met Laban's eager gaze with a gentle firmness. "The gifts are indeed valuable," he conceded, his voice steady, "but they are but a reflection of the true value my master sees. He seeks not merely a bride for his son, but a daughter for his house, a woman of character, of kindness, and of a spirit that mirrors the divine favor that has guided our paths."

He then turned his attention to Bethuel, his words carrying a weight of sincerity that transcended mere earthly considerations. "Abraham's desire is for a union built on love, on mutual respect, and a shared understanding of faith. He has entrusted me with the delicate task of finding a young woman whose heart is as

86

pure as the water she draws, whose spirit is as steadfast as the ancient stones, and whose disposition reflects the grace of the heavens. He believes, with all his being, that the Lord has guided my steps to this place, to you, and your family."

Rebekah listened, her heart swelling with a complex mixture of emotions. While Laban and her father focused on the material and societal implications, her spirit resonated with Eliezer's emphasis on character and divine guidance. The thought of being chosen, not just for her family's sake, but for who she was, for the qualities Eliezer had so eloquently described, filled her with a quiet joy. The earrings and bracelets were beautiful, yes, but the true treasure, she felt, lay in the unspoken promise of a life lived in purpose, in faith, and the embrace of a loving God.

There was a brief, yet significant, pause as Bethuel and Laban exchanged a look. The family's dynamics were clear: Laban, the younger, more impulsive one, was driven by ambition; Bethuel, the patriarch, was more measured, weighing the pronouncements of a stranger against the established realities of their lives.

"Your words are profound, traveler," Bethuel finally said, his voice thoughtful. "Abraham's reputation precedes him, and the sincerity of your mission is evident. However, this is a matter of great consequence, one that involves not just our family, but the future of our daughter." He looked at Rebekah, his gaze filled with a father's love and concern. "Rebekah, my child, this man speaks of a life far from here, of a son you have never met. What are your thoughts? Your heart has always been your truest guide."

The question hung in the air, a moment of intense scrutiny. All eyes turned to Rebekah. She felt a blush creep up her neck, not entirely from shyness, but from the sudden, intense focus of her family's attention. She looked at Eliezer, at the earnest hope in his eyes, and then at her father and brother, their faces etched with anticipation, albeit for different reasons.

"My father," she began, her voice clear and steady, though a tremor of emotion still lingered within it, "Eliezer speaks of a path guided by God. He has seen me draw water, and he has seen kindness. If it is indeed God who has led him here, and if these qualities are what Abraham seeks for his son, then... then my heart is not closed to it." She paused, gathering her courage, her gaze meeting Eliezer's directly. "The gifts are beautiful, and the prospect of joining a family of such faith and standing is... significant. But more than the gold, it is the conviction in Eliezer's words, the mention of God's will, that speaks to me."

Laban, however, interjected, his voice brimming with practicality. "Rebekah, this is not just about feelings. This is about the future! Think of the security, the prosperity! Abraham's household is blessed. Isaac will undoubtedly inherit vast wealth. This is an opportunity to elevate our family, to ensure a life of comfort and influence for generations to come." He gestured towards Eliezer with an almost aggressive enthusiasm. "We must consider this seriously, Father. This is not merely a proposal; it is a divine decree presented with tangible proof of Abraham's sincerity."

Bethuel held up a hand, quieting his son. He understood Laban's perspective, the desire for material advancement, but he also recognized the deeper currents at play. Eliezer's tale was woven with threads of faith, of a covenantal promise that extended beyond mere earthly riches.

"Indeed, Laban," Bethuel replied, his voice measured, "prosperity is a blessing, and Abraham's blessings are well known. However, a marriage is a union of souls, not just of fortunes. Eliezer, your master Abraham has presented a compelling case, one that touches upon matters of deep spiritual significance. However, before we can provide a definitive answer, we need to gain a better understanding of the situation. We must ensure that this union is indeed what the Almighty intends, and that Rebekah's heart is truly in accord with this path."

He turned back to Eliezer, his gaze serious. "You have spoken of your journey, and the signs that guided you. You have presented gifts that speak of Abraham's esteemed position. But you have also spoken of a profound faith, a trust in divine providence. I wish to understand this more deeply. Tell us, Eliezer, how can we be certain that this is not merely a matter of worldly aspiration, but a true calling, a partnership blessed from above?"

Eliezer inclined his head, acknowledging the weight of Bethuel's question. He understood the need for reassurance, for a shared understanding of the divine mandate. "Bethuel," he began, his voice resonating with a deep, unwavering conviction, "the signs are not merely in the gold, nor the lineage of Abraham, though these are significant. The true sign is in the *heart* of the one who is sought. Abraham's prayer was not for a woman of wealth or status, although these qualities may have been present. His prayer was for a woman of selfless character, of unwavering kindness, of quiet dignity, and of a spirit that would honor God and walk in His ways. He prayed for a woman who would be a true companion, a nurturer of faith, a pillar of strength for his beloved son."

He looked directly at Rebekah, his gaze gentle but unwavering. "When I saw Rebekah at the well, I saw the answer to that prayer. I saw a young woman who, despite the arduous task, offered water not only to me but to my weary beasts. I saw a spirit of boundless generosity, a quiet strength that spoke of inner resilience, and a modesty that belied her inherent worth. These are not qualities that can be bought or faked; they are woven into the very fabric of a soul touched by divine grace. Abraham's quest is not for a mere bride, but for a daughter of God, a woman who embodies the virtues that will ensure a righteous lineage and a life of blessed purpose."

He paused, allowing his words to settle. "The confirmation, as Abraham envisioned it, lies in Rebekah's response. If her heart is open, if she feels a resonance with this calling, then we have the most powerful sign of all – the liberty of a willing spirit, guided by the same divine hand that led me here. It is not my place to force or to persuade beyond revealing the truth of Abraham's intent and the evidence I have found. The decision, ultimately, rests with Rebekah, and with the wisdom of her family."

Bethuel listened intently, his expression unreadable for a moment. He saw the sincerity in Eliezer's eyes, the depth of his conviction. He also saw the conflict within his son, Laban, whose focus remained primarily on the material benefits. And he saw his daughter, Rebekah, whose quiet gaze held a profound thoughtfulness, a reflection of a heart already weighing the spiritual implications of Eliezer's words.

"Rebekah," Bethuel said again, his voice softer this time, turning to his daughter. "You have heard Eliezer. You have heard your brother's enthusiasm and my reflections. The path he proposes is one of great change, of leaving behind all that is familiar for an unknown life, albeit one with promise. Does your heart truly feel drawn to this, not just by the gifts or the potential for advancement, but by the spirit of the call itself?"

Rebekah took a deep breath, the weight of her family's gaze pressing upon her. She looked at the gold in her hands, then at Eliezer, the emissary of this extraordinary proposal, and finally, she met her father's eyes, her own filled with a newfound resolve. "Father," she said, her voice steady and clear, "I have always believed that God guides our lives. Eliezer has spoken of

Abraham's faith and a divine plan. The journey he describes is indeed far from home, and the man I am to meet is a stranger. But the qualities Eliezer has seen in me, the qualities he says Abraham seeks – kindness, generosity, steadfastness – these are the things I have always strived for. If it is God's will that I should join Isaac, Abraham's son, then I am willing to journey. My heart feels a stirring, a sense that this is a path I am meant to walk. I accept this proposal, with the understanding that it is guided by faith."

A collective exhale seemed to ripple through the small gathering. Laban's face lit up with undisguised delight, already imagining the benefits. Bethuel, though still contemplative, showed a flicker of paternal pride in his daughter's thoughtful response. Eliezer, for his part, offered a subtle nod, a gesture of quiet gratitude and relief. He had presented the proposition, had laid bare the sincerity of Abraham's intent, and now, Rebekah, with her family's blessing, had embraced the possibility.

"Then it is settled," Bethuel declared, his voice firm with decision. "We will prepare for your departure, Rebekah, and for the engagement that will follow. Eliezer, you have brought us tidings of great import. We will host you with the honor due to your mission and your master."

As Eliezer began to detail the following steps, the practicalities of arranging the journey and the formal betrothal, Rebekah felt a profound sense of peace settle over her. The initial shock and bewilderment had given way to quiet acceptance, a deep-seated certainty that she was moving according to a higher purpose. The doubt, the familial discussion, the weighing of earthly benefits against spiritual conviction–it had all served to solidify her resolve. She looked at the gold in her hands, no longer just a symbol of wealth, but a tangible representation of a divinely orchestrated beginning, a wellspring of providence from which a new life was about to flow. The journey from the well had been short, but the path it had opened stretched out before her, vast and filled with the promise of a destiny she was now ready to embrace.

Now, preparing to leave and saying goodbye to her family, probably for good, would be the most challenging part.

# Chapter Five:

# The Journey to Rebekah's New Home

Eliezer, his posture radiating a newfound solemnity, turned to Bethuel, the patriarch of this humble yet significant household. The air thrummed with anticipation, the recent acceptance from Rebekah having solidified the extraordinary nature of the moment. He held Rebekah's gaze for a fleeting instant, a silent acknowledgment of the courage and faith she had displayed. Then, he addressed Bethuel directly, his voice imbued with the weight of his master's trust and the gravity of his mission. "Bethuel," he began, his tone resonating with a deep sincerity that commanded attention, "the Lord has indeed guided my steps to this place, and He has shown me, through Rebekah's spirit and your family's character, the answer to a prayer that has been on Abraham's heart for many years."

Eliezer's eyes then shifted, encompassing both Bethuel and Laban, as he elaborated on the hopes Isaac's father held for his future spouse. "Abraham's heart's desire, and indeed Isaac's as well, is for a companion who will not only share his life but will also nurture the divine spark within him, and within the family they will build. He seeks a woman who embodies the virtues that Rebekah has so clearly demonstrated: kindness that flows not from obligation but from a generous spirit, hospitality that extends to stranger and beast alike, and a quiet strength that can weather life's storms with grace. He seeks a wife who will be a true partner, a confidante, and a mother whose influence will shape righteous descendants, continuing the legacy of faith and obedience that has been so painstakingly established."

He then looked towards Rebekah, his gaze holding a profound respect. "Rebekah, your willingness to embark on this journey, to embrace this calling, is a testament to the very qualities Abraham seeks. You are not merely being chosen as a bride for Isaac; you are being invited to become the matriarch of a lineage that God Himself has promised to bless immeasurably. You are to be the one who will bring comfort to Isaac after his mother's passing, the one who will share in his life's joys and burdens, and the one who will help carry forward the sacred covenant. This is not a light undertaking, nor is it a simple arrangement of marriage. It is a calling, a divine mandate that binds two souls together for a purpose far greater than themselves."

Bethuel listened intently, his weathered face a study in contemplation. He understood the weight of Eliezer's words, the significance of a son of Abraham seeking a wife from their lineage. He had seen the potential, felt the divine touch in Eliezer's narrative, and

94

now, his daughter's willingness had sealed the immediate decision. Yet, he also recognized the immense responsibility that lay ahead of him. He looked at Rebekah, his heart swelling with a mixture of pride and a father's inherent protective instinct.

"Eliezer," he responded, his voice steady and measured, "you have laid before us a proposition of great consequence, one that speaks of divine favor and a future that stretches beyond our immediate understanding. We see the sincerity in your words, and Rebekah has shown a spirit that aligns with the virtues you describe. But for us, as a family, and for Rebekah as an individual, the weight of this decision is immense. What are the assurances that this union will indeed be a source of blessing, and what are the responsibilities that will fall upon Rebekah and our family?"

Laban, ever eager and pragmatic, chimed in, his voice tinged with excitement and a keen awareness of the opportunities presented. "Indeed, Eliezer. Abraham is renowned for his wealth and his favor with God. Isaac will undoubtedly inherit a vast estate. To have Rebekah, our sister, become the wife of such a man, to have our family connected to such a prominent and blessed household— it is an honor beyond measure. We understand the blessings that will flow, not only to Rebekah and Isaac but also to our own family. What are the specific terms of this arrangement? How will our family benefit from this sacred connection?" His gaze, though respectful, held an unmistakable glint of anticipation for the tangible rewards that lay ahead.

Eliezer addressed Bethuel's concerns with calm reassurance. "Bethuel, the assurance of blessing lies not in earthly wealth alone, though Abraham's prosperity is indeed a testament to God's favor. The true assurance lies in the unwavering commitment of Abraham and Isaac to uphold the covenant and to honor God in all their dealings. They seek a partner who shares this commitment—a woman who will be a co-heir in God's promises. Rebekah, as Isaac's wife, will be cherished and honored. She will be a central figure in the household, not merely a servant but a companion and a co-ruler in the domestic sphere. She will be entrusted with the nurturing of Isaac's well-being and the raising of their children in the ways of the Lord."

He then turned his attention to Laban's more material questions. "As for specific terms, Laban, Abraham is a man of immense generosity. He has already provided a generous dowry in the form of these precious gifts, which are but a token of his true intent. Upon Rebekah's arrival, she will be welcomed into a household of abundance, and her needs and those of her future children will be more than adequately met. The true benefit, however, is not merely material. It is a spiritual inheritance, a participation in a lineage blessed by God, and an opportunity to contribute to a family whose very existence is a testament to divine faithfulness. Abraham has tasked me not only with finding a wife for Isaac but also with ensuring that this union is a harmonious and blessed one, reflecting the principles of faith and love that govern his own life."

Eliezer continued, his words painting a vivid picture of the life Rebekah would lead and the role she would play in it. "Isaac has been sheltered, yes, but not in a way that has made him weak or dependent. His upbringing has been one of discipline, of learning the responsibilities of leadership, and of understanding the importance of stewardship. He has learned from Abraham the values of justice, mercy, and integrity. He is now ready to take a wife, build a home, and continue the legacy of his father. Abraham envisions Rebekah not just as a bride, but as the future matriarch of this blessed house, a woman whose wisdom and godliness will guide their family for generations to come. She will have a significant voice in household matters, her counsel will be valued, and her influence will be felt throughout the community."

He looked at Bethuel again, seeking to address any lingering doubts. "This is not a matter of coercion or forced obligation, Bethuel. It is an invitation, extended through divine providence, for Rebekah to step into a role of profound significance. Abraham's desire is for a willing heart, a joyful acceptance of this calling. "

Rebekah, who had been listening with rapt attention, felt a surge of understanding and a deepening sense of purpose. The initial awe and the family's deliberations had been intense, but Eliezer's detailed explanation of Isaac's character and the envisioned role for her as matriarch resonated deeply within her. It wasn't just about marrying a man of wealth or a prominent family; it was about being part of something divinely ordained, a continuation of a sacred trust. She looked at her father and brother, seeing the flicker of acceptance in their eyes, the dawning realization of the magnitude of the opportunity.

Bethuel, after a moment of thoughtful silence, nodded slowly. "Eliezer, your words carry the weight of truth and sincerity. We have seen the hand of God in your coming, and Rebekah's spirit has responded affirmatively. We understand the significance of this union, not just as a marriage, but as a fulfillment of promises made by the Almighty. We entrust our daughter to you, and through you, to Abraham and Isaac, with the prayer that this partnership will be blessed abundantly, and that Rebekah will indeed find joy and purpose in her new home."

He then turned to Rebekah; his gaze filled with fatherly love and a quiet blessing. "My daughter, you have made your choice with wisdom and faith. Go, and be a blessing. We will prepare you for your journey, and our hearts will be with you, praying for your safe passage and your happiness."

Laban, catching his father's sentiment, stepped forward, his earlier focus on material gain now tempered by a genuine affection for his sister and a nascent understanding of the spiritual significance. "Rebekah," he said, his voice softer than usual, "may your journey be swift and your welcome warm. Remember us, and know that our family stands with you in this momentous step." He then turned to Eliezer with renewed respect. "Eliezer, we are honored by your presence and by the tidings you have brought. We will ensure that all is prepared for Rebekah's departure, and that she goes forth with the blessings of our household."

Eliezer bowed his head in gratitude. "Bethuel, Laban, your trust and your daughter's willingness are deeply appreciated. Abraham will be overjoyed to hear this news. We will make arrangements for the journey with haste, and all will be done with the utmost respect and care for Rebekah. The days ahead will be filled with preparation, and I will guide you through each step, ensuring that Rebekah's transition is as smooth and as filled with joy as Abraham himself would desire."

He then turned back to Rebekah, a gentle smile gracing his lips. "Rebekah, your acceptance is the greatest gift Abraham could have received. Prepare yourself for a journey of faith, a journey that will lead you to a life of purpose and profound blessing. You are embarking on a path that has been divinely ordained, a path that will shape not only your destiny but the destiny of many to come."

He then elaborated on the journey itself, emphasizing the need for Rebekah to be accompanied by her attendants. These women would provide comfort and familiarity during the long travel and her initial days in a new land. This was a crucial aspect, as Eliezer understood the emotional toll of such a significant move and wanted Rebekah to feel supported and cared for from the very beginning. Eliezer detailed the provisions that would be made for their comfort and safety, ensuring that Rebekah would be treated with the honor and respect due to the future wife of Isaac, and indeed, as a daughter of Abraham's household. The itinerary, he explained, would be carefully planned to ensure a safe and timely arrival, allowing ample time for rest and acclimatization.

The conversation then shifted to the betrothal ceremony itself. Eliezer explained that, according to Abraham's instructions, a formal covenant would be established, binding Rebekah and Isaac in a covenant before God and their community. This was not merely a cultural formality, but a sacred commitment —a testament to the seriousness and sanctity of the union. He outlined the symbolic gestures that would accompany the betrothal, reinforcing the spiritual nature of their bond. He conveyed Abraham's heartfelt desire for Rebekah's family to be involved in every step, to witness the commitment, and to share in the joy of this auspicious occasion.

Bethuel, listening to Eliezer's detailed plans, felt a profound sense of peace settle over him. He saw the meticulousness with which Eliezer approached his task, the genuine care for Rebekah's well-being, and the profound respect he had for his family. He knew, with an unshakeable certainty, that his daughter was being sent into a life of purpose and honor, guided by a faith that mirrored his own most profound convictions. He readily agreed to all of Eliezer's proposals, assuring him that their family would work diligently to prepare Rebekah and to participate fully in the betrothal ceremony.

Laban, too, was fully engaged, his earlier avarice having transformed into a sense of fraternal pride and responsibility. He saw the immense importance of this union and the legacy it represented, and he was eager to ensure that his sister was sent forth with the full blessings and support of their family.

As the discussions drew to a close, Eliezer presented Rebekah with a final, precious gift from Abraham: a delicate, intricately carved ivory comb, a symbol of refinement and beauty, and a small, leather-bound book containing selections of Abraham's wisdom and prayers, a testament to the spiritual foundation of the household she was to join.

"Rebekah," Eliezer said, his voice filled with warmth, "this comb is a reminder of the beauty that resides not only on the outside but also within. And this book—this holds the wisdom that has guided Abraham, the prayers that have sustained him through trials, and the promises that are now yours to embrace. May they be a constant source of comfort and strength as you embark on this new chapter."

Rebekah accepted the gifts with a humble heart, her eyes shining with emotion. The weight of the ivory comb was light, but the weight of the book, filled with her future father-in-law's legacy, was immense, representing the spiritual inheritance that was now within her grasp. The journey home from the well had indeed been a journey towards destiny, and the proposal, now formally accepted, was the momentous first step in fulfilling a promise that would echo through the ages.

Rebekah stood, her heart aflutter with a mixture of trepidation and a profound sense of purpose. The air in her father's home, once filled with the mundane rhythms of daily life, now crackled with the weight of an extraordinary decision. Eliezer's words, recounting Isaac's gentle spirit, his devotion to the Almighty, and the immense spiritual heritage he represented, had woven a tapestry in her mind – a vision of a life far removed from the familiar fields and the comforting embrace of her family. Yet, it was not merely the prospect of a life of ease or prestige that drew her. It was the quiet certainty that had settled deep within her soul, a knowing that this path, though unknown, was the one divinely appointed for her.

She had seen the sincerity in Eliezer's eyes, heard the truth resonate in his voice, and felt the undeniable touch of the divine in his narrative.

Her family, too, had grappled with the magnitude of the proposal. Bethuel, her father, a man of deep faith and quiet wisdom, had wrestled with the paternal instinct to keep his daughter close, to shield her from the uncertainties of a distant land and an unknown future. Yet, he had also recognized the unmistakable hand of God at work. Eliezer's arrival, his respectful demeanor, and the divine assurance he carried were undeniable. He saw in Rebekah's contemplative stillness the same quiet conviction that mirrored his faith. Laban, her brother, initially swayed by the allure of Abraham's wealth and influence, had also been touched by the spiritual gravity of the moment. The prospect of his sister becoming a cornerstone of a lineage blessed by the Most High was an honor that transcended material gain.

"My daughter," Bethuel's voice, though weathered by years of labor, held a resonance of unwavering love and support, "your heart has spoken, and we have heard its quiet conviction. While the thought of your departure brings a pang to my soul, the greater assurance is knowing that the Almighty guides your steps. You are not merely leaving a home; you are stepping into a destiny prepared for you by the One who sees all and knows all." He looked at her, his gaze a testament to years of shared laughter and quiet understanding. "Go, Rebekah. Go with our blessing, with our prayers, and with the unwavering knowledge that you carry the heart of this family with you. May your journey be safe, and may your new life be filled with the joy and purpose that the Lord has ordained."

Laban, his earlier boisterousness replaced by a profound tenderness, stepped forward, placing a hand on her shoulder. "Rebekah, sister," he said, his voice thick with emotion, "though the miles will separate us, the threads of our lives remain intertwined. You have always been a source of light and strength in our home, and I know you will shine brightly in your new one. Do not forget us, but most importantly, do not forget the God who has brought you to this place. We are proud of the courage you possess, and we eagerly await the stories of the blessings that await you." He offered a smile, a shared memory of their childhood passing between them. "May your path be smooth, and may you find a love as deep and enduring as the wellsprings from which you drew your strength."

Eliezer, witnessing this tender exchange, felt a profound sense of gratitude wash over him. The reluctance inherent in any family's parting with a beloved member was palpable, yet a powerful faith and a genuine recognition of the divine orchestration tempered it.

"Rebekah," he began, his voice gentle, "Abraham entrusted these to me as tokens of his profound respect and anticipation. This book contains not just his wisdom, but the very words that have sustained him through countless trials, as well as the prayers that have formed the bedrock of his life. It is a testament to the spiritual heritage you are now a part of. And this comb," he indicated the intricately carved ivory, "is a symbol of the beauty that adorns the faithful, a beauty that radiates from a heart submitted to God's will. Let them serve as constant reminders of the covenant you are entering, a covenant built on faith, obedience, and the promises of the Almighty." Rebekah accepted the gifts with a reverence that belied their physical lightness.

The preparations for her departure were swift, undertaken with a blend of solemnity and joyful anticipation. The family, united in their purpose, worked together to gather the necessary provisions for Rebekah's journey. Fine linens, woven with care by her mother's hands, were packed alongside sturdy, practical garments for travel. Provisions of dried fruits, grains, and preserved meats were carefully selected to ensure her comfort and sustenance.

Her mother, her eyes often brimming with unshed tears, worked with a quiet determination, ensuring that Rebekah would lack for nothing essential. There were discussions among attendants about ensuring she had companions who would offer familiarity and support in the unfamiliar lands she would soon traverse. Eliezer, ever-present and guiding, offered his counsel, ensuring that Rebekah's needs were met with utmost consideration and respect.

"It is crucial," Eliezer explained, his voice steady, "that Rebekah is not only well-provisioned but also well-accompanied. I have brought women who can offer her comfort and help her. However, her companions (girls her age) are essential to help her share in conversations and provide the familiar rhythms of home during this significant transition. These ladies will be treated with honor and respect, both when we arrive and throughout our stay.

Bethuel, his voice softening, acknowledged Eliezer's comments and replied, "It is a long journey, and the world beyond our familiar lands is vast and sometimes uncertain. But we have placed our trust in the Almighty, and He has provided you, Eliezer, as a guide and protector for her on this path."

Laban, his hands busy sorting through the various items, added, "And we will ensure that she has provisions not just for her body, but for her spirit as well. We will include scrolls of our family stories, songs that have been passed down through generations, so that a part of home always remains with her, no matter how far she travels." His eyes met Rebekah's, a shared understanding passing between them. He was not just sending his sister away; he was entrusting her to a greater purpose, a destiny woven with threads of faith and divine promise.

The actual departure day dawned clear and bright, a stark contrast to the emotional weight that hung in the air. Rebekah, dressed in her finest travel attire, stood before her family, a figure of quiet grace and newfound resolve. The gifts from Abraham lay carefully packed, ready to be carried alongside her belongings. The ivory comb was tucked into a small pouch, a comforting reminder of the promise of beauty and refinement. The book of wisdom was secured within her traveling satchel, a spiritual anchor for the journey ahead.

Her mother embraced her, her tears finally falling, wetting Rebekah's cheek. "My precious daughter," she whispered, her voice choked with emotion, "may the Lord watch over you and keep you. Remember all that you have been taught, and never stray from the path of righteousness. Your father and I will carry you in our hearts, always."

Bethuel held her close, his strong arms a symbol of the protection she had always known. "Be brave, my child," he murmured, his voice rough with feeling. "Your faith is your strongest shield. Trust in it, and trust in the One who leads you."

Laban, after another firm embrace, stepped back, a flicker of wistfulness in his eyes. "Write to us, Rebekah, when you can. Tell us of your journey, of Isaac, of your new home. We will await your words like rain in a dry season." He then turned to Eliezer, his demeanor respectful and assured. "Eliezer, we entrust our sister to your care. May her journey be blessed, and may she arrive safely in Canaan."

Eliezer bowed his head, accepting their trust with the solemnity it deserved. "Bethuel, Laban, your faith and your love for Rebekah are a testament to your character. I pledge to you that she will be treated with the utmost honor and respect, and her journey will be conducted with all the care and attention that Abraham himself would provide. She is not merely a bride; she is a precious gift, a vital part of a promise that spans generations."

As Rebekah mounted the waiting camel, surrounded by her chosen attendants and the provisions meticulously prepared, she looked back one last time at her family. They stood together, a tableau of love and sacrifice, their faces etched with a mixture of sorrow and pride. Her mother waved her hand, which trembled slightly. Her father stood tall, his gaze steady, offering a silent blessing. Laban offered a final, encouraging nod, his smile conveying a depth of unspoken affection.

With a gentle nudge from Eliezer, the caravan began to move, leaving behind the familiar landscape, the comforting scent of home, and the wellspring that had been the backdrop to her childhood. The journey ahead was long, spanning vast distances and crossing unknown territories. But as Rebekah settled into her saddle, the leather-bound book of wisdom close at hand, she felt no fear, but a quiet anticipation. She was not merely traveling to a new land; she was embarking on a sacred quest, a journey of faith towards a destiny divinely orchestrated, a destiny that would see her become a cornerstone of a lineage blessed by the Almighty, a matriarch whose story would be woven into the very fabric of salvation history.

The choice had been made, the blessing given, and the journey home, paradoxically, was leading her further than she had ever imagined, towards a future illuminated by the unwavering light of God's promise. The desert sands stretched before her, vast and silent, mirroring the immense unknown that lay ahead, yet within her heart, a quiet certainty bloomed – the conviction that she was walking in step with God's perfect plan. This was not just a departure; it was an ascension, a stepping into the grand narrative that the Creator had set in motion, a narrative in which she was destined to play a pivotal role.

The camel's gentle sway was a rhythm all its own, a cadence that would soon become as familiar to Rebekah as the rustling of the olive trees near her childhood home. The caravan, a small but determined procession, had finally set out, leaving behind the familiar, comforting embrace of her father's homestead. The air, initially thick with the bittersweet ache of farewell, had begun to thin as the miles stretched between them and the cherished faces they had left behind. Rebekah, perched atop her mount, a soft woolen shawl draped over her shoulders against the morning chill, stole a glance backward. The figures of her father, Bethuel, and her brother, Laban, grew smaller against the expansive canvas of the landscape, their forms eventually blurring into the dust kicked up by the caravan's progress. Her mother's final wave, a fragile flutter of white fabric, was still imprinted on her mind's eye, a poignant visual testament to the love that propelled her forward.

Eliezer, riding on a camel beside her carriage, was reassuring. He understood the profound transition Rebekah was undergoing. He had witnessed countless journeys in his service to Abraham, but each one carried its unique significance, its intricate tapestry of hopes, fears, and divine purposes.

"And what of the route, Eliezer?" she inquired, her voice steady despite the tremor in her heart. "Are there particular points of interest or challenges we should anticipate?"

Eliezer's eyes scanned the horizon, a seasoned traveler assessing the path ahead. "Our journey will take us through familiar territories initially, then across the plains and towards the foothills leading to Canaan. We will generally follow established trade routes, ensuring our safety and access to water sources. There will be days of intense sun, and nights under a canopy of stars that I suspect you have never witnessed before, Rebekah. We must be mindful of the heat, the potential for sandstorms, and the need to rest the animals adequately. But I assure you, Abraham has spared no expense in ensuring our comfort and security. He has made arrangements with trusted individuals along the way who will provide us with fresh supplies and safe resting places."

As the caravan moved further from her home, the landscape began to shift subtly. The familiar fields gave way to rolling hills, then to sparser vegetation. The air grew drier, carrying the scent of dust and distant blossoms. Rebekah found herself observing the world with a new intensity. The flight of a hawk, the subtle changes in the color of the earth, the way the sunlight caught the edges of the distant mountains—all of it was data, impressions of a world far larger and more complex than she had previously known.

After a while, they stopped for the women to stretch and attend to their personal needs. While stopped, one of the women, a kindly older woman that Eliezer had brought with him, named Hannah, approached Rebekah with a steaming cup of a fragrant herbal infusion. "Drink this, daughter," she said softly, her voice warm and melodic. "It will refresh you and help you settle into the rhythm of the journey."

Rebekah accepted the cup, the warmth seeping into her hands. The taste was subtle, earthy, and slightly sweet, a welcome comfort. "Thank you, Sarah," she replied, offering a small smile. "It is very soothing."

Hannah settled down beside her, her eyes crinkling at the corners. "It is a great honor to be chosen to accompany you, Rebekah. We will try to answer any questions you have about Abraham's household and the blessings that flow from it." She gestured to the book in Rebekah's lap. "That book... it holds the wisdom of a man who walked closely with God. I have heard tales of his unwavering faith, his hospitality, and his profound connection to the Divine. Now, you can read it for yourself. It was written by Abraham's own hand."

"Indeed," Rebekah murmured, her fingers brushing against the worn leather. "Eliezer spoke of it. He said it contains Abraham's prayers, his thoughts. I am eager to learn from it." It was a rare quality that Rebekah could read. It was not customary for women to be afforded the luxury of an education, but Bethuel had insisted that Rebekah learn all that she could. He wanted her to one day inherit their lands and business with her brother Laban. To not be beaten by her older brother, Bethuel knew she would need to be able to read. Bethuel had no idea that God was giving him this insight and desire because he had a plan for Rebekah that was much more elaborate than anything Bethuel could have dreamed.

As the day wore on, the sun climbed higher, casting long shadows that shortened and then disappeared as midday approached. The caravan paused in the shade of a small grove of acacia trees, allowing the animals to rest and the travelers to partake in a midday meal. Rebekah shared a simple repast of dates, bread, and cheese with her attendants and Eliezer, the conversation flowing easily, a gentle blend of practical concerns and shared observations. Eliezer recounted stories of Abraham's early life, of his unwavering trust in God during times of famine, war, and personal hardship. He spoke of the deep, abiding love Abraham had for his son, Isaac.

"Abraham's prayers for a wife for Isaac were fervent and specific," Eliezer explained, his voice carrying the weight of a deep spiritual conviction. "He prayed not for riches or status, but for a woman of godly character, a woman who would honor the Almighty and uphold the principles of our covenant. When I saw you, Rebekah, I saw that prayer answered. I saw the same quiet strength, the same deep reverence for God, that defines Abraham and Isaac themselves."

Rebekah listened intently, a sense of awe washing over her. To think that her life, her very being, was the

108

answer to such a profound prayer, a prayer offered with such earnestness by a man of Abraham's stature, was humbling beyond measure. It was a confirmation, a validation of the divine hand that had guided Eliezer to her home and had opened the hearts of her family to this momentous undertaking.

The journey continued, day after day, under the vast, indifferent sky. The rhythm of the caravan became a familiar lullaby. Rebekah learned to gauge the passage of time by the position of the sun, the changing patterns of the stars at night, and the subtle shifts in the desert flora and fauna. She spent hours reading the book of Abraham's prayers, finding solace and inspiration in his words. His humble petitions, his expressions of gratitude, his unwavering faith in the face of adversity—they resonated deeply with her own developing understanding of God's presence in her life. She saw how Abraham's faith was not a passive thing, but an active, living force that shaped every aspect of his existence.

One evening, as the caravan settled down for the night, the air cool and crisp after the heat of the day, Rebekah sat outside her tent, gazing up at the countless stars that dusted the velvet sky. The silence of the desert night was profound, broken only by the occasional bleating of a sheep or the soft murmur of conversation from the other tents. Eliezer joined her, sitting a respectful distance away, his gaze turned towards the celestial expanse.

"It is a vastness that can be both intimidating and comforting," Eliezer observed, his voice low. "It reminds us of our smallness in the grand scheme of things, and yet, it also testifies to the immense power and majesty of the Creator. It is in such moments that Abraham often found his deepest connection to God."

Rebekah nodded, her heart filled with a quiet reverence. "I feel it too," she confessed. "A sense of awe, and a deep peace. It is as if the very silence speaks of His presence." She turned to Eliezer, her expression earnest. "Tell me more about Isaac. What is he like? What are his passions, his dreams?"

Eliezer's face softened as he spoke, "Isaac is a man of deep character, Rebekah. He mirrors his father's gentle spirit and his unwavering devotion to the Almighty. He is a man of prayer, of quiet contemplation, and immense integrity. He finds joy in the simple rhythms of life, in the tending of the flocks, and in the fellowship of those who walk with God. He carries the weight of Abraham's legacy with a profound sense of responsibility, and he longs for a companion who will share his faith, his devotion, and his vision for the future." He met Rebekah's gaze, his eyes conveying a sincere belief. "I have no doubt, Rebekah, that you are the one chosen to bring him solace, joy, and a partner in his sacred calling."

Rebekah absorbed his words, picturing Isaac as Eliezer described him. A man of faith, of gentleness, of devotion—these were qualities that resonated deeply within her own heart. The prospect of sharing her life with such a man, of building a future together in the land of promise, filled her with a quiet, profound hope. The journey, with all its challenges and its beauty, was not just a physical passage; it was a pilgrimage of the heart, a moving towards a destiny that felt both divinely ordained and deeply personal.

As the stars wheeled overhead, Rebekah felt a growing certainty that she was not merely traveling to a new home, but stepping into the embrace of a love that was as ancient and as enduring as the very heavens above. The parting from her family had been difficult. Still, the promise of what lay ahead—a life woven into the grand narrative of God's covenant—was a beacon that illuminated her path, guiding her ever onward toward Canaan and the man who awaited her. The farewells, though tinged with sorrow, were ultimately overshadowed by the vibrant certainty of a future shaped by divine love and purpose.

"The route we take now will lead us through the foothills," Eliezer explained, his voice a calm counterpoint to the rustling of the camel's harness. "It is a land of stark beauty, Rebekah, where the earth breathes with an ancient scent. The air will be drier, the sun more insistent, but the vistas are unlike any you have seen. You will see mountains that wear crowns of stone and valleys that cradle hidden springs." He gestured towards the undulating terrain that stretched before them. "It is a land that tests, certainly, but it also rewards those who persevere. It reminds one of the strength that lies dormant within, waiting to be called forth, much like the deep roots of the desert shrubs that cling tenaciously to life."

Rebekah listened, her gaze sweeping across the ever-changing panorama. The vastness that had once seemed daunting was slowly transforming into a source of quiet wonder. She saw the resilience in the sparse vegetation, the enduring spirit in the ancient rock formations. It was a landscape that demanded respect, a testament to the enduring power of nature, and in its way, a reflection of the God who had sculpted it. Eliezer's words about dormant strength resonated deeply. She felt it stirring within her, a quiet determination born of purpose and an unspoken faith in the path unfolding before her.

"Abraham often spoke of the peace he found in these lands," Eliezer continued, his eyes fixed on the distant horizon. "He found a profound connection to the Almighty amidst the silence and the grandeur. He would often sit for hours, simply observing the sky, the earth, and the creatures that moved through them. In that quiet contemplation, he would hear the whispers of divine guidance. He believed that God's presence was woven into the very fabric of creation, and that by attuning ourselves to the natural world, we could better discern His will." He glanced at Rebekah, a gentle smile gracing his lips. "I believe you possess that same sensitivity, Rebekah. You have a quiet spirit, a deep well of introspection that will serve you well as you prepare to join Isaac's household."

The compliment, offered with such genuine sincerity, brought a warmth to Rebekah's cheeks. She felt the truth in Eliezer's observation. The solitude of the journey, the vastness of the sky above, had indeed opened a new channel of awareness within her. She found herself more attuned to the subtle shifts in the wind, the calls of unseen birds, the very texture of the air. It was as if the journey itself was a spiritual discipline, stripping away the superficial and revealing the core of her being.

As they progressed, Eliezer began to weave tales of Isaac's life in Canaan, painting a picture of a man shaped by his father's legacy and his deep devotion. "Isaac is a man of deep faith, Rebekah, much like Abraham, though his path has been different. Abraham's journey was one of pioneering, of forging new paths in unfamiliar lands. Isaac's is one of tending, of nurturing, of building upon the foundations his father laid. He oversees the flocks, the lands, and the household with a gentle hand and a keen understanding. He is a man of peace, not given to boastfulness or outward show, but possessing a quiet strength that commands respect."

He paused, allowing his words to settle. "He has known trials, of course. The famine that once afflicted this land tested even Abraham's faith, and Isaac, even as a young man, bore witness to the unwavering trust his father placed in God. He learned early on the importance of perseverance, of leaning not on human strength, but on the ever-present power of the Almighty. And he carries that lesson within him, a deep-seated understanding of where true security and sustenance lie."

Rebekah listened, her imagination filling in the details of Eliezer's descriptions. "He is a man who values wisdom and faithfulness above all else," Eliezer continued, his gaze earnest. "Abraham's greatest hope, and Isaac's deepest desire, is to see this covenant, this sacred promise, continue to flourish."

The weight of Eliezer's words pressed upon Rebekah, not as a burden, but as a confirmation of her purpose. As the days melted into a harmonious rhythm of travel, Rebekah found herself increasingly comfortable in Eliezer's company. The initial formality had softened, giving way to a shared understanding and mutual respect. They spoke of their families, of their hopes, of the lessons life had taught them. Eliezer, in turn, shared more intimate details about the customs and daily life in Canaan, preparing her for the cultural nuances she would encounter.

"In Canaan," Eliezer explained one evening, as they sat by a small, controlled fire, the desert night air cool and fragrant with the scent of distant herbs, "life is structured around the rhythms of the land and the teachings of our fathers. Hospitality is paramount. A stranger is not merely welcomed; they are honored. It is a cornerstone of our way of life, a reflection of Abraham's renowned generosity. You will find that wells are communal gathering places, where news is exchanged and bonds are strengthened. The care of the flocks is a communal effort, with much of the day spent in watchful tending and peaceful communion with nature."

He continued, his voice thoughtful, "The women of the household play a vital role. They manage domestic affairs, prepare food, weave garments, and nurture the young. There is a deep respect for their contributions and a recognition of the spiritual strength they bring to the family unit. While Isaac's primary responsibilities lie in overseeing the larger affairs of the household and the

113

lands, the women ensure the smooth functioning of daily life, creating a sanctuary of peace and order. Abraham's household, in particular, is known for its spiritual depth, with prayer and thanksgiving being a constant feature of each day."

Rebekah absorbed these insights, her mind meticulously cataloging the information. She understood that her role would be significant, a partnership that extended beyond companionship to encompass the spiritual and practical stewardship of Abraham's legacy. The emphasis on hospitality, on community, and on the vital role of women in maintaining the household's well-being resonated deeply with her innate values.

"You will find that Isaac's mother, Sarah, although she has now been called home to be with the Lord, was a woman of immense faith and dignity," Eliezer added, his tone softening with remembrance. "Her journey was one of quiet strength, of unwavering trust in God's promises, even in the face of doubt and hardship. Isaac carries her spirit within him, her quiet resolve, and her deep devotion to the Almighty. He learned from her the importance of patience and the knowledge that God's timing is always perfect."

He met Rebekah's gaze, his expression earnest. "Abraham's love for Sarah was a testament to a bond forged in faith and loyalty. And in seeking a wife for Isaac, Abraham desired a woman who would embody similar virtues—a spirit of devotion, a willingness to nurture, and a heart that beat in rhythm with the divine will. He did not seek a woman who would merely fill a space, Rebekah, but one who would enrich the covenant, a true partner in the continuation of God's plan."

Rebekah felt a profound sense of connection to this lineage and the unfolding narrative. The stories Eliezer shared were not mere anecdotes; they were threads woven into the fabric of her destiny. She saw the echoes of Abraham's faith in Isaac, and she felt a growing

114

certainty that she, too, was called to participate in this sacred continuity. The journey was no longer just a physical passage; it was a spiritual pilgrimage—a deliberate movement toward a life of purpose and deep, abiding faith.

As they neared the borders of Canaan, the landscape began to change more dramatically. The rolling hills gave way to more rugged terrain, the vegetation becoming sparser yet more resilient. The air grew even drier, carrying the scent of dust and the faint, sweet perfume of unseen desert blooms. Eliezer pointed out landmarks, sharing the historical and spiritual significance of each place, further grounding Rebekah in the land she was about to call home.

"This is the land that God promised to Abraham and his descendants," Eliezer declared, his voice filled with a reverent awe as they crested a particularly high ridge, revealing a breathtaking vista of valleys and distant, sun-drenched plains. "A land flowing with milk and honey, a land that will be a testament to the faithfulness of our God. It is a land of blessings, but it is also a land that requires a steadfast heart and an unwavering spirit. Abraham faced many challenges here, but through it all, his faith never faltered."

Rebekah felt a tremor of emotion surge through her. The reality of her impending arrival, of meeting the man who was to become her husband, was becoming increasingly palpable. The conversations with Eliezer, along with the stories of Isaac and his family, had transformed abstract anticipation into tangible hope. She saw the journey not as an ending, but as a profound beginning, a stepping stone into a life rich with spiritual purpose and the promise of a deep, shared love.

The parting from her family had been a sorrowful necessity, but the burgeoning certainty of a future interwoven with divine intention and the prospect of a life united with a man of God's choosing filled her heart with a quiet, yet profound, anticipation. The landscape stretched before them, a canvas of promise, and as the steady pace of the camels kept their comforting rhythm,

Rebekah closed her eyes and said a prayer of thanks to this God of Abraham's for her safe journey. "God, I want to know you like Abraham does. Please reveal yourself to me and teach me how to honor you. I know that you are the god I was searching for and longing for as a child back home."

One evening, as the last vestiges of sunlight bled from the sky, he spoke, his voice carrying a new resonance. "We are drawing nearer, Rebekah, to the heart of this land. To the place where Abraham established his covenant, and where Isaac now dwells." He paused, letting the weight of his words settle into the stillness of the desert night.

Rebekah listened, her heart swelling with a mixture of emotions. The apprehension she had initially carried—a quiet tremor of the unknown—was steadily being replaced by a burgeoning sense of peace. It was not a passive peace, but an active one, a quiet confidence born from the assurances Eliezer had offered and the deep sense of purpose that had blossomed within her. The thought of meeting Isaac, the man whose life she was to join, was no longer a distant, abstract concept, but a tangible prospect, imminent and real.

As the days progressed, Eliezer began to speak more specifically of Canaan, the city that lay ahead, and the area that the merchants called Gaza, where their massive compound was located.

Eliezer described the people she would be interacting with daily. He spoke of their daily lives, their devotion, and how the city itself seemed to breathe with a spiritual vitality. "Our compound and village," he continued, "is a reflection of your journey, Rebekah. It is where the ancient foundations of Abraham's faith meet the vibrant unfolding of the present. It is where the legacy of the past is honored, and where the future is built upon those enduring principles. Just as you have journeyed from your homeland, leaving behind the familiar, you are now approaching a place that bridges the old and the new, a symbol of the continuity that defines our people."

Rebekah found herself drawn to his descriptions. She envisioned the compound Eliezer depicted, a place of both strength and life, a testament to resilience and enduring faith. The idea of her future home and village as a symbol of her transition resonated deeply with her. She was, in essence, a bridge herself, connecting he life she had known with the one that awaited her.

Eliezer, sensing her engagement, continued to offer reassurance regarding Isaac. "You may feel a touch of apprehension as we draw closer," he acknowledged, his tone gentle and understanding. "It is natural to feel a degree of trepidation when facing such a significant turning point. But I assure you, Rebekah, Isaac is a man of profound gentleness. His heart is as vast and as open as the plains we have traversed. He has been shaped by his father's wisdom and his deep devotion to the Almighty. He is not a man of harsh words or demanding spirit, but one who leads with kindness and a quiet strength."

Eliezer spoke of Isaac's daily life, of his meticulous care for the flocks, his dedication to the stewardship of Abraham's lands, and his unwavering commitment to the principles of righteousness. "He finds joy in the simple rhythms of life," Eliezer explained, "in the tending of the sheep, in the quiet contemplation of God's word, and the anticipation of a life shared with a faithful companion. He has been prepared for this moment, just as you have. He longs for a partner who will share not only his life but also his spirit, a woman who understands the importance of faith and the blessings that flow from a life lived in accordance with God's will."

**117**

The anticipation in the air was no longer just a feeling; it was a palpable presence, a humming energy that seemed to permeate the very atmosphere. As they drew closer to Canaan, the landscape began to shift, the sparse vegetation giving way to more cultivated fields, the signs of human habitation becoming more frequent. The distant silhouette of the city, its ancient walls rising against the azure sky, began to sharpen into focus. Rebekah's gaze was drawn to it, a mixture of awe and eager expectation filling her heart. This was the threshold, the gateway to the life that had been so carefully orchestrated by divine providence.

Eliezer observed her with a quiet satisfaction in his eyes. He had carried the weight of this mission with a solemn dedication, and now, as its fulfillment drew near, he felt a profound sense of gratitude. He had witnessed God's hand at work, guiding their steps, providing for their needs, and preparing Rebekah for this pivotal role. The faithfulness of God, a theme that had woven itself through every aspect of their journey, was now approaching its tangible realization. He felt the stirring of a profound peace, a quiet joy that came from seeing a divine plan come to fruition.

Rebekah felt certain that Gaza, the surrounding areas, and their compound were a spectacular display of ancient grandeur. The anticipation of living there grew with every mile they traveled. At first, she thought this month-long journey would be tiresome, but now she was extremely grateful for the extended time. She was feeling more comfortable every day. She was going to know everything possible about her future husband by the time she arrived. She was fortunate to have Eliezer, who provided her with numerous valuable insights. It was as if she were getting a 15-year betrothal's worth of knowledge about her future husband.

# Chapter Six:

## *Meeting Her Soul Mate*

---

The sun was slowly rising until noon today. It appeared to be on a faster descent. Almost as if it recognized that there was something special for the afternoon, and it had to get there quickly.

Isaac had told his servant earlier in the morning that he had a special feeling about today. I have been wondering for a couple of weeks now if each day would be the day she arrives. But today is different. I feel something in my bones. I have this ache in the pit of my stomach. My heart is racing today. I keep feeling like I hear a voice saying, "Today, be ready. Today, my son, get ready."

His servant, Aziah, was smiling at him. "Master, I feel it too. I have been awake since before dawn. I feel it so strongly that I want to hurry up and get our chores done so that we can go for a long afternoon walk in that far northeastern pasture. We could see the caravan when it came down that last mountain pass. It would take about four hours to reach us at that point. So, we would have enough time to get the women cooking and making the final preparations in Sarah's tent for her."

"Sounds like a deal, Aziah," chirped out Isaac, and he was off before he finished the sentence! There was a lot to do and many chores, but today they would get done quickly. Aziah knew that because Isaac was singing and whistling this morning!

Isaac thought they would never get done. But at last the last animal was fed and watered. He ran back to his tent to get a bath and put on clean clothes. Aziah was there helping him. As soon as Isaac was dressed, he turned around to Aziah. "I should make a note in my journal while I have the time. You bathe and put on your best uniform. I want you bright and shining. I do not want her to think we are nomads—even though we are— she will be the queen of this village and compound. She needs to be greeted as one. Off you go—get ready!"

While Isaac was waiting for his servant, he took out his journal. It was a rare and expensive binding of Egyptian parchment that Abraham had gotten for his 16th birthday. He began that day by writing down anything unique, special, or life-changing that happened. Most of the entries he gave a title to, so he could quickly glance back through the pages and find notes. This leather-tied binding was holding three hundred pieces of Egyptian parchment. The journal was so big, he did not worry about anyone stealing it, because most of the servants could not read or write. This book was too heavy to carry around, but he had documented all special events in his life since the day he got this gift. This type of parchment was rare due to its thinness and silky finish. The pages were extra-large, measuring larger than the registration books he had seen at the town meetings that recorded land purchases and transfers.

He titled the page "Preparing to Meet My Bride." Before he could finish listing what he wanted prepared for the feast the night of his bride's arrival, Aziah was back, polished and spit-shined, with clean sandals and clothes. " Master?" He pipped, grinning from ear to ear, "I am ready,

Isaac did not need to be asked twice. Yes, he was ready! Let us get two of the camels, so we have a place to sit while we wait for her. Plus, we can follow the caravan back. I hope you are bringing both camels back, because she lets me ride with her.

Aziah, with his young, keen eyes, saw the caravan first. Isaac told him what he wanted for the meal, had him repeat it twice, then sent him running back to the compound on his camel. Issac told him to get the servant girls preparing the tent and the cooks with their apprentices working at maximum speed. They would have at most four hours to prepare. He instructed Aziah to return to him as soon as instructions were given and his father had been told.

Isaac knew that Abraham would need a couple of those hours to get himself cleaned up and ready. Plus, he would have things he wanted added to the "to-do list" for the servants and cooks, Isaac was certain.

It felt like it was taking forever for them to make it across the plains. What are they doing? Don't they realize that they need to be at the compound before dark? When he was about to give up, he heard the familiar beating of the camel's hooves on the dry path. Thank God, Aziah is going to be back!

Isaac was so stiff and tired, he dismounted from his camel as soon as Aziah had arrived. He told Aziah, "Let us go for a stroll toward the road that comes in here.

Our land goes for another mile after you pass that bend in the road. I do not know if we can make it all the way there. There may be rocks and bramble in our way, but let us walk as far as we can. I cannot wait to get a glimpse of her!

Isaac and Aziah were about a half mile from the bend when the caravan came into sight. All of a sudden, it came to an abrupt stop. Isaac said, "Aziah, why on earth are they stopping? I hope there is nothing wrong. That is our camels right? The sun is so low that it is making a shadow across the caravan, and I cannot see."

A couple of minutes passed, and Aziah went laughing and jumping up and down. "Master, she is coming, she is coming!"

"What do you mean she is coming, Aziah?" Isaac cried, "Jumping goats, Aziah, you are going to give me a heart attack. I cannot see. What is she doing?"

"She is running toward us, Master! She is young, thin, and beautiful!"

---

Rebekah has talked us to death today. She started like a bird chirping, Eliezer, as soon as they got on the camel. She refused to ride in the carriage with the girls who had accompanied her on this trip. She promptly told Eliezer, "That camel saddle on your camel will handle two people easily without me touching you. So, I want to ride with you."

The sun will blister you; you must stay in the carriage so you are covered. That is not necessary. I will cover my head and face with a scarf. I know we are going to be there this afternoon. I want to be able to see where we are going to live, and I want to be the first one to see my Isaac. You have told me so much, but I have more questions for you today. I need to be where we can talk all day. I want to be ready when he comes out to greet

122

us." Rebekah was bursting with so much energy that Eliezer could not say no.

"Okay, you can ride up here until we get to the compound. I will have to stop and let you get back in the caravan. It would not do for any of the servants or my wife to see you raiding up her with me." He firmly told her.

"It is a deal. I promise!"

That may have been her first words that day, but it was not her last. Several times, Eliezer had silently prayed that she would get tired and want to lie down. When he realized that was not going to happen, he began to pray she would shut up! He knew that women asked too many questions!

Eliezer was telling Rebekah that they were nearing their destination. "You see that bend in the road? When we get there, we will stop. You can see the beginning of the compound property from that bend. I do not want anyone to see us stopping. Therefore, it would be safer if we stop there and make the changes to the carriage. Additionally, the women will need to help you clean up and remove the dust from your clothes, so that you will be ready for a brief meeting. You will then have time to get properly cleaned up and ready for the evening meal. I left instructions for your tent (Sarah's Tent) to be ready for you."

They stopped, and before Rebekah dismounted, she saw two figures walking in the field to their right. Who is that? Are the workers for you, or is that someone else's land? Eliezer looked up, and to his shock, it was Isaac and Aziah. Oh, no, he was in trouble.

"Oh no, that is Isaac and his manservant, Aziah. Down, Rebekah, quick, you must get into the carriage before they see you. I am in so much trouble, hurry!" Eliezer begged.

Like lightning, Rebekah was off the camel. However, she did not go toward the camels carrying the carriage for the women; she was off running like a deer across that field. How in the world did she get over that fence so quickly, Eliezer thought. I thought she was more mature than this—Isaac is going to be upset that I have brought back someone that he will have to wait a few years before he can marry. "Oh God help me," Eliezer begged.

---

Isaac and Aziah were situated amidst the gentle slopes near the foothills northeast of Gaza. He was in the northernmost part of the land that Yahweh had promised Abraham. It was now week fourteen since Eliezer had left to embark on the task of finding him a wife. He had come out this way to get a glimpse of the caravan when it arrived.

Issac and Aziah had been gradually working their way out to this far end of the fields all week. Isaac used the excuse that he needed to observe the work and check on the servants in this area to make sure that they were not in any danger from the Amalekites, who were only 30 miles north of there.

He was Abraham's son, heir to a legacy of faith, of covenants, and of promises that stretched back to the very dawn of their lineage. His father's teachings were deeply etched into his soul, a constant compass guiding his steps. He had learned the importance of unwavering trust in the Almighty, of the profound significance of every word spoken by God, and of the sacred duty to uphold the principles of righteousness. Now, with his father's servant away on a mission of utmost importance, Isaac found himself in a period of reflective waiting. The task entrusted to the servant resonated deeply within Isaac's own heart—the search for a wife, a partner to share not just his life, but the spiritual inheritance passed down through generations.

Isaac's days had not been spent idly waiting these 14 weeks, but in diligent stewardship. He walked among his father's herds, his touch gentle, his knowledge of each animal intimate. He understood the land, its seasons, its challenges, and its blessings. This was his inheritance, and he tended to it with the same reverence his father had shown. Yet, even amid these practical duties, his mind often drifted to the purpose of the servant's journey. He trusted implicitly in his father's wisdom, in his discernment, and, above all, in his profound connection with the Divine. Abraham had assured him that God guided this endeavor, and in that certainty, Isaac found a deep well of peace.

He remembered the countless conversations with his father, discussions that often turned to the future, to the continuation of their family and the fulfillment of God's promises. Abraham had spoken of the importance of a wife who would be more than a companion; she would be a partner in faith, a woman whose spirit would align with the covenant, whose heart would beat in rhythm with the divine purpose that had shaped their lives. Isaac yearned for that connection, for a shared understanding that transcended mere earthly bonds. He prayed not for a specific face or form, but for a woman chosen by God — a woman who embodied the qualities his father had described: faithfulness, kindness, and a deep reverence for the Almighty.

He knew that his father had provided detailed instructions for the servant, including specific signs to look for and a clear understanding of the qualities that would mark the chosen one. These were not arbitrary requirements, but indicators of a heart aligned with God's will. Isaac felt a quiet confidence that the servant, a man of proven loyalty and profound spiritual understanding, would faithfully carry out Abraham's wishes. He had witnessed firsthand the servant's devotion, his unwavering commitment to his master and to the God they both served. There was no doubt in Isaac's mind that this mission was in capable hands, guided by a wisdom that surpassed human understanding.

The nights in the desert offered a spectacle of unparalleled beauty. The sky, unburdened by the artificial lights of cities, blazed with a million stars, each one a distant spark in the infinite darkness. Isaac would often gaze at them, feeling a sense of awe at the grandeur of creation and a profound connection to the generations who had stood beneath the same celestial canopy, their hearts lifted in prayer and contemplation. He saw in the enduring light of the stars a metaphor for the enduring nature of God's promises, a constant presence in the ever-changing cosmos.

His thoughts would inevitably turn to the woman he was to meet. He imagined her journey, her hopes and perhaps anxieties, as she too embarked on a path guided by providence. He prayed for her protection, for her strength, and for her heart to be open to the path laid out for her. He understood that this was not merely a matter of family alliance or personal preference; it was a sacred undertaking, a continuation of a covenant established with Abraham and now being extended through him.

The days blurred into a gentle succession, each one bringing him closer to an unknown but anticipated moment. He continued to fulfill his responsibilities, his faith serving as a constant anchor. He found solace in the familiar routines, in the quiet meditations, and in the deep trust he placed in his father and God. He was a man rooted in the earth, his feet firmly planted in the land he was to inherit, yet his spirit soared, reaching for the divine assurances that filled his days with purpose.

Now, his thoughts are being interrupted by Aziah's screaming. What had possessed this servant?

Then Isaac's eye caught a glimpse of what Aziah was looking at—the most beautiful creature he had ever seen—she was running toward him like she was flying on angel wings. For a moment, Isaac thought his heart was beating in his head, not his chest. Oh no, I am going to pass out, he thought. Then Aziah grabbed his arm and said, "Come on, Master. We need to meet her. It is not fair for her to run all the way."

With that tug, Isaac was in motion. When Isaac and Rebekah met, there was a brief pause, and they stood looking at each other in shock.

Aziah was the first to regain composure. "My dear, we need to help you get back to the caravan. It is too far to walk to the compound. It is a long camel ride."

"I feel like walking, what do you think, Isaac?"

"I would love to walk and talk, but it will be dark soon, and the snakes and camel spiders are bad in this area. I do not want anything to happen to you. We will walk and talk until Eliezer gets the caravan over here to us. He will have to take that path around. That will give us some time. Let us start walking toward the path," and Isaac pointed toward a clearing about a mile away.

Rebekah readily agreed, and then she said, "Oh, I know Eliezer will give you my ancestry, family history, and the details of how he chose me over the evening meal. I have had five weeks of riding to get here. I have questioned Eliezer with everything I can think of about you. I know that is not fair because you do not know anything about me. But we have a year for you to learn about me. What I want to know before we meet everyone else is if you like me, like what you see, and if you are willing to spend time with me, teaching me what it is that God wants me to do for you and this family. All of my life, I have felt that I was destined for something different. I have always felt that I would live somewhere far away. Additionally, I have been a thorn in my parents' side

127

because I have questioned everything they tried to teach me about all our gods. I was always asking them, what if there is a god that we do not know about—what then? Oh, my, see, I am rambling on. I forgot to tell you my name. I am Rebekah. I am from Norah near Ur of the Chaldeans and Mesopotamia."

Isaac was smiling with a grin that could have lit up an entire tent without the need for candles or oil. This 14-year-old's energy level, compared to his already settled 40-year-old self, was refreshing, but also reminded him that he was getting old. Glad she had the energy for children, he thought to himself!

---

At this point, they had reached the path, and Eliezer was approaching. He was apologizing extensively for Rebekah's outburst. He asked forgiveness of Isaac and promised that he would finish his instructions with her over the next couple of weeks, then have his wife and the other women begin working with her for the wedding and feast prep.

Isaac patted Eliezer on the arm and replied, "Eliezer, my faithful servant, do not worry. There was no harm done. I am so glad to see that she is not dreading being married to an old man. Glad she has so much energy. I can use this in my life right now. You know how depressed I have been since Momma died. This is a good thing. I look forward to hearing about your journey, including how you selected her and the agreements you made with her family. However, we need to return to the compound and get you settled in. I have the cooks making a celebration meal for tonight. You can tell us first about meeting her and her family. Then you can share tidbits of the journey with us over the next few weeks during the evening meal. I will need you and your wife to join us each

night. I will need help with her and her companions. I
see you have brought several with you."

---

The bell began to ring to call everyone to the
evening meal that was being prepared outside of Abraham
and Sarah's tents. Isaac's tent was close by, but across the
path.

Rebekah had rushed to get ready. There was not
much time for fancy fixings and four-hour hair styles. The
meal was finishing as they rode up. But she was eager to
have time with Abraham and Isaac.

As everyone gathered around the low table that
was prepared for them to sit at, cushions, blankets, and
pads were laid out for their comfort. It was going to be
an exciting meal.

Abraham motioned to everyone where to sit.
Then he placed Rebekah and her traveling companions
close to him and Isaac on their right side. He placed
Eliezer and his wife on his left side. Then all the servants
and individuals helping with the journey were also allowed
to enjoy the special meal. They were seated at a table away
from the main table, but still close enough to hear what
was being said. Even though they had been on the
journey, they had not been privy to all communications,
agreements, and questions. This was new information to
them as well.

After Abraham had everyone seated and served,
he asked Eliezer to stand and give them a brief report of
what had happened. More details could follow later. An
overview was all that was needed tonight. He and Isaac
were aware that everyone was tired and needed rest.

As Eliezer stood up before Abraham's household
to give his report, he suddenly realized how weary he was
from this journey. But when he started talking about the

anointing and the favor God placed on him, he caught a second wind, and his weariness melted away!

Initially, the air crackled with an unspoken tension. However, as his report began to be delivered, the tension shifted to eagerness and apprehension about what was to come next. It was almost midnight, and no one wanted to leave. He realized he had been talking for a couple of hours now. He should have been tired, but with love in the air—all of that changed!

Eliezer explained, "I come to you this day not merely as your servant, but as a witness to the remarkable providence of the Almighty. The journey I undertook was one of immense significance, a quest to find a wife for our beloved Isaac, a woman who would not only be a companion but a true partner in the covenant that binds us to God." He paused, allowing the gravity of his words to settle. "And I stand before you now, with a heart overflowing with gratitude, to declare that the Lord has not only guided my steps but has, in His infinite wisdom, revealed to me a woman whose very spirit is a reflection of the divine qualities we sought."

Eliezer then recounted the intricate details of his arduous journey. He spoke of the caravans he joined, the vast distances he covered, and the myriads of people he encountered along the way. He described the bustling marketplaces of distant cities, the quiet contemplation found in remote encampments, and the ever-present challenge of discerning God's will amidst the cacophony of human affairs. His narrative painted a vivid picture of a world far removed from the serene landscapes of Beersheba. In this world, the covenant's promises were tested against the backdrop of diverse customs and beliefs.

"My journey led me to the city of Nahor," Eliezer continued, his voice gaining a measured cadence. "As you instructed, Master Abraham, I prayed diligently at the well outside the city as evening approached, the time when the women of the city would come out to draw water. It was a time of seeking, a moment to present my plea to the Lord, asking Him to direct my path and to grant me a sign through which I might identify the woman He had chosen for Isaac." He described the ritual of his prayer, the earnestness with which he pleaded for divine intervention, and the deep sense of responsibility he felt in fulfilling Abraham's charge.

"And then, she appeared," Eliezer's voice softened, a hint of wonder entering his tone. "A young woman, of striking beauty, indeed, but it was not her outward appearance that first captured my attention. She approached the well with a grace and purpose that set her apart. Her name, I soon learned, was Rebekah, the daughter of Bethuel, son of Milcah, whom you mentioned, Master Abraham, as a potential connection through our lineage." A murmur of recognition rippled through the gathered crowd. Isaac felt a jolt of something akin to recognition himself, a premonition that this woman's story was intrinsically linked to his destiny.

Eliezer then detailed the encounter at the well, the very moment for which he had prayed. "As I watched, she lowered her pitcher to the well, and I approached her. I asked her, 'Please, give me a little water from your pitcher to drink.' Her response, Master Abraham, was not one of hesitation or demand, but of immediate, selfless generosity. She not only lowered her pitcher for me to drink, but she added, 'I will draw water for your camels also, until they are finished drinking.'"

The significance of this simple act was not lost on Eliezer, nor on those who heard him. He elaborated on the immense labor involved in drawing water in such a place, and the extraordinary kindness shown by Rebekah. "These were not just words, but a demonstration of a willing and generous spirit. Offering water to a stranger is an act of hospitality. Still, offering water to his camels as well —a task that requires considerable effort and time—

revealed a depth of character that far surpassed mere politeness. It was a virtue that spoke volumes of her upbringing and the inherent goodness of her heart."

He continued, recounting how he offered her a golden earring and two bracelets as a token of his appreciation, and how she readily accepted them. He then cautiously revealed his identity and his purpose, asking if there was room in her father's house for him to spend the night. "Her reply," Eliezer stated, his voice resonating with the truth he had witnessed, "was immediate and welcoming. She said, 'I am the daughter of Bethuel, the son of Milcah, whom Abraham's servant is seeking.' This confirmation, following her unparalleled act of kindness, was the sign I had so earnestly prayed for. It was as if the heavens themselves had opened, confirming that this was indeed the one chosen by God."

Eliezer's narrative then shifted to the events that followed his arrival at Rebekah's home. He described the hospitality he received from her family, including her brother Laban. He recounted how he presented his master's request, laying out the details of Abraham's vision and the continuation of the covenant. "I explained to Bethuel and Laban the purpose of my journey, the blessings that awaited Isaac and his chosen bride, and the solemnity of the covenant we uphold. I presented the gifts that Master Abraham had entrusted to me, not as a price, but as a testament to the honor and respect we held for their family and for the woman God had chosen."

He then spoke of Rebekah's response. "When I inquired if she would go with me, her father and brother, after a night of deliberation, yielded to the undeniable signs of God's hand. They acknowledged that this was a matter ordained by the Almighty. And when they asked Rebekah, 'Will you go with this man?' she did not falter. With unwavering conviction, she replied, 'I will go.'" Eliezer emphasized the courage and faith displayed by Rebekah in making such a life-altering decision, leaving behind her family and her homeland for a future yet unknown, guided only by divine confirmation.

"Her willingness to depart with me, without hesitation, was another profound testament to her faith and her trust in the Lord's plan," Eliezer continued. "She understood, as I had explained, that this was not a mere marriage arrangement, but a sacred joining, a continuation of a divine lineage. Her heart was open to God's will, and she embraced this destiny with a grace that left me utterly convinced of her suitability."

Eliezer then described the journey back, taking care to ensure Rebekah's comfort and protection. He spoke of the joy and relief that filled his heart with each passing day as they drew closer to Beersheba. He painted a picture of Rebekah as a woman of remarkable composure and quiet strength, even as she journeyed towards an entirely new life. "She inquired about Isaac, her future husband," Eliezer recounted, "and I shared with her all that I knew of his character, his devotion to God, and the righteous path he walks. I assured her that he was a man of deep faith and integrity, a worthy heir to Abraham's legacy."

The climax of Eliezer's report was the arrival at Beersheba. He described the scene as they approached, the familiar landscape now imbued with even greater significance. "As we neared the pastures, Isaac himself was out in the field, meditating as the day began to cool. It was a moment of profound anticipation, the meeting of destinies that had been set in motion by divine decree and the steadfast faith of Master Abraham." Eliezer's eyes met Isaac's, a silent communication passing between them – a shared understanding of the magnitude of this moment.

"When Rebekah saw Isaac, she dismounted from the camel and asked Eliezer, 'Who is this man walking in the field to meet us?' Upon hearing, 'It is my master,' she quickly veiled herself. This gesture, Master Abraham, was one of respect and humility, acknowledging Isaac's status and her role as his intended bride. It was a silent affirmation of the sanctity of their impending union." Eliezer's voice was filled with conviction. "And as Isaac led her into the tent of Sarah, his mother, and took Rebekah to be his wife, and loved her, he was comforted after his mother's death. This, I believe, is the fulfillment of the promise, the beginning of a new chapter in the covenant, guided by the hand of God Himself."

Eliezer concluded his report with a heartfelt declaration of his certainty. "Master Abraham, I have witnessed firsthand the character of Rebekah, her virtue, her kindness, her unwavering faith. I have seen how God has orchestrated every step of this journey, from the initial prayer at the well to her willing acceptance of this sacred calling. I am not merely reporting my findings; I am testifying to the divine intervention that has brought us this woman. She is, without a doubt, the one chosen by the Almighty for Isaac, the one who will carry forward the promises made to our father, Abraham."

The entire household listened in rapt attention, a profound sense of peace and confirmation settling upon them. Eliezer's detailed account left no room for doubt. His narrative, rich with the evidence of God's guidance and Rebekah's exceptional character, resonated deeply within each person. Isaac felt a profound sense of peace wash over him, a calm assurance that the woman now standing beside him was indeed the one he was meant to be with.

The anxieties and uncertainties of the waiting period dissolved, replaced by a quiet joy and a deep gratitude for God's faithfulness and Eliezer's diligent service. Abraham's vision was being realized, the covenant was being honored, and a new era was dawning upon their lineage, guided by the light of divine providence and the remarkable virtue of a woman named Rebekah. The servant's report was not just a recounting of a journey; it was a testament to faith, a declaration of divine appointment, and the heartwarming confirmation that destinies, indeed, had met.

Abraham and Isaac listened to Eliezer's report, absorbing every word of the incredible journey and the virtuous woman who had answered the call. Yet, hearing of her and seeing her, even from afar, were two entirely different realities. He had faith, a faith that had been tested and affirmed countless times, but this was a moment that transcended mere belief; it was the precipice of a life divinely ordained.

A profound sense of gratitude washed over Isaac. Gratitude for his father's unwavering faith, for Eliezer's diligent service, and for the divine hand that had guided them all to this point. He felt a deep sense of peace, a quiet joy that pulsed through him, mirroring the serenity of the desert landscape around him. This was not merely the culmination of a journey; it was the beginning of a shared pilgrimage.

With the completion of Eliezer's report, Isaac turned to Rebekah and her companions. "Tomorrow, we will tour you through the compound and show you where things are located. We will finalize housing for your companions. Tonight, all of you will sleep in the same tent with Rebekah."

"Bear with us," he continued, "We will make sure that your needs are met and you are comfortable. I am so sorry that we were not prepared for your arrival. I am happy that Eliezer agreed for you to come. Dad and I did not even think about that—we sent female servants to help Rebekah—but friends her age were also important.

Then Issac escorted the ladies to Sarah's tent. As he approached it, he looked at Rebekah and said, "This is where your accommodations will permanently be—close to Dad and me for safety reasons. He saw Rebekah's eyes survey the tent, a flicker of appraisal, but more importantly, a look of quiet acceptance.

Their conversation, though brief in its initial exchange, was already weaving a tapestry of understanding. Isaac found himself drawn to Rebekah's calm demeanor, the way she listened with a quiet intensity that suggested a depth of thought. He saw no artifice, no pretense, only a genuine spirit ready to embrace a new life. He felt a deep gratitude for the journey she had undertaken, a journey of faith that mirrored his own. He offered her a small, genuine smile. "It is good to see you here," he said, his voice softer now, more personal. "The journey has been long, and I know the desert can be a harsh companion, but I pray you will find solace and joy in this place. Get in, get some rest. Do not worry about rising early. Tomorrow needs to be a day of rest for all of you. We will meet again over the evening meal to hear more about the journey. I will arrange for tours and instructions at a later time in the next couple of days. I just realized how tired you guys are right now. Your health is more important! So, rest!"

Rebekah felt her apprehension melt away with each passing moment. Isaac's demeanor was one of profound kindness, his eyes reflecting a gentle spirit that put her at ease. She saw in him a man of maturity and quiet strength, someone who carried the weight of his lineage with grace. As she looked at him, the initial nervousness she had felt upon arriving began to dissipate, replaced by a growing sense of belonging. It was as if the prayers of her kin and the faith that had propelled her forward had culminated in this gentle, reassuring presence. "Thank you," she replied, her voice steady, "Your welcome and concern is a comfort after such a long journey."

Isaac nodded, a warmth spreading through him that had nothing to do with the desert sun. He saw in Rebekah's response a confirmation of the qualities Eliezer had so enthusiastically described. There was a quiet dignity about her, a self-possession that was both striking and deeply comforting. He felt an undeniable pull, a sense of recognition that transcended mere visual appraisal. It was as if a long-held anticipation was finally being met, not with fanfare, but with a profound, quiet understanding. "Rebekah, I am grateful that you have answered the call and come to join me on this journey of life."

The tent, when Rebekah entered, was a sanctuary of soft light and woven textures. Eliezer had overseen its preparation with meticulous care, ensuring it was a haven from the desert's embrace. The air inside was still, carrying the subtle scent of dried herbs and something faintly floral—a welcome contrast to the dry, dust-laden atmosphere outside. Cushions of rich fabric were arranged invitingly, and a low table held earthenware vessels, likely filled with refreshments and plenty of water. Was everyone here as thoughtful and helpful as you?

As Rebekah settled onto one of the cushions, her movements were fluid and unhurried. She looked at him, and in her eyes, he saw a reflection of the same quiet anticipation that had settled within his soul. "It is a beautiful space," she replied, her voice soft but clear. "Thank you, Isaac. You and your father have shown me such kindness." Her words were simple, yet they carried a weight of sincerity that resonated deeply within him. He found himself captivated by the genuine nature of her gratitude, the absence of any pretense or expectation.

With simple goodbyes, Isaac and Abraham left the tent. The ladies were so glad to be alone, finally. The cushions and bed were calling them with a magnetic pull—was it possible for a human to survive the weight of tiredness, Rebekah wondered.

### The next day:

The women of the household, in particular, found themselves drawn to Rebekah's gentle nature. They saw in her a kindred spirit, someone who understood the nuances of building a home and nurturing a family. They brought her gifts, small tokens of welcome and affection – intricately woven cloths, fragrant oils, and polished stones that spoke of the land's bounty. Rebekah received each offering with sincere gratitude, her eyes shining with a genuine appreciation that disarmed any formality. She saw not just the gifts themselves, but the spirit in which they were given, a spirit of sisterhood and shared purpose that made her feel instantly at ease, as if she had always belonged.

Isaac watched these interactions with a quiet joy, recognizing the nascent bonds of community that were already forming around Rebekah. He saw her engaging with the women, listening attentively to their stories, her responses marked by a gentle warmth and an innate kindness. It was clear that she possessed a gift for connecting with people, for making them feel seen and valued. This, he knew, was a precious quality, one that would enrich their lives and strengthen the fabric of their household. He felt a deep pride in the woman who had captured his heart, a woman whose character was as radiant as the desert sun.

Isaac had cancelled all of his plans for the day. He felt that he needed to stay near the tent for at least the first seven days. He needed to be close and ensure that she was settled, knew who to contact, and where to go. He took every opportunity to get near her all day.

Now it was time for the evening meal again. Oh, how patiently he was waiting for the opportunity to enjoy the evening meal and have this interaction with her?

As the week rushed by, Isaac could not believe that he would have to go back to work so soon. Where

138

had time gone? Now that she was settled, the wedding preparations would begin. Additionally, they would need to consider the ideal timing for the ceremony, taking into account her young age and maturity level.

On the second day of rest (second Sabbath or Shabbat), Rebekah reached over and touched Isaac's hand and said something that made his heart flip. When he got back to his tent, he rushed to his journal to make an entry. He wrote.

*Rebekah survived the arduous journey and faced the uncertainty of the unknown, giving up all that she had ever known to travel here and be with us, because it was God's will. Today, she said a new realization had dawned upon her. She said ....Isaac, I am home!*

*Yahweh, you have been so good to me! Thank you*

"Isaac and Rebekah" by La Wanda Blackmon

## Chapter Seven:

# *Love's Enduring Foundation*

---

The initial days of their union settled upon Isaac and Rebekah like a warm, familiar cloak, woven from threads of mutual respect and a shared reverence for the divine. Their life together began not with grand pronouncements or earth-shattering events, but in the quiet rhythm of shared days, each one a gentle affirmation of their covenant. They lived in the verdant lands of Canaan, along what is now known as the Gaza Strip. Their compound was a place that offered both sustenance and solace, a canvas upon which their life together would be painted.

Each time they cuddled up on the pillows at night to discuss their day, somehow their conversations always drifted back to Rebekah's 40-day (five weeks and four days) journey from Ur. Rebekah's memories were now starting to fade as she and Isaac were building memories together. However, a familiar smell or reaction from an animal would remind Rebekah of something that she wanted to share with Isaac.

Isaac rolled over tonight and looked at Rebekah with a playful look in his eyes. "Dear, you realize that we keep extending the amount of time it takes for us to go to sleep by about 15 minutes each night. We have more and more to discuss. Guess it is going to take us over 12 hours to get ready for bed and cover our days by the time we have a couple of kids!" he said, laughing. Rebekah slapped his arm and said, "I am not that long-winded! I have a lot to catch you up on, and I have many questions for you. It will get better, my love! AT least we like talking to each other—that is more than most newlyweds can brag about.

Both of them were so content with the profound contentment in the simple acts of their married life. He would rise before the sun, his spirit already attuned to the blessings of a new day, and often, he would find Rebekah already awake, her presence a quiet comfort in the pre-dawn stillness. They would share a few words, a prayer of gratitude offered together, before the duties of the day called them. He observed her with an ever-deepening admiration, noticing the grace with which she moved through their dwelling, the quiet efficiency with which she managed the household tasks, and the genuine warmth she extended to all who crossed their path. She brought an order and a serenity to their home that resonated deeply within him, a harmonious counterpoint to the sometimes-demanding nature of their pastoral life.

Rebekah, in turn, discovered in Isaac a partner whose spirit mirrored her own. His devotion was not ostentatious, but a steady, unwavering presence that underscored every aspect of his being. She saw in his eyes the same deep faith that guided her steps, a faith that was not a burden, but a source of strength and a constant reminder of their shared purpose. He respected her thoughts, counsel, and deeply held convictions, creating an environment where her voice was not only heard but also valued. This mutual deference was the invisible mortar that strengthened the walls of their union, ensuring that their shared life was built on a foundation of true partnership.

Their days were filled with the shared responsibilities of a life intertwined with the land. They worked side by side, tending to the flocks, overseeing the fields, and managing the affairs of their households. There was a natural synergy in their collaboration, a tacit understanding that allowed them to anticipate each other's needs and to work with a harmonious efficiency. Isaac would often find Rebekah discussing household matters with him, her insights sharp and practical, her perspective always grounded in a wisdom that seemed to flow from a deep wellspring of discernment. He would listen intently, valuing her input and recognizing that their combined efforts were far greater than the sum of their contributions.

The quiet joys were manifold, woven into the fabric of their everyday existence. They found pleasure in shared meals, where conversation flowed easily, punctuated by laughter and a deepening of mutual understanding. They found solace in each other's company during the peaceful evenings, watching the stars emerge in the vast desert sky, a silent testament to the enduring power of creation. Isaac would often recount stories of his father, Abraham, of the trials and triumphs of his faith, and Rebekah would listen with rapt attention, her own experiences of faith weaving into the narrative, creating a tapestry of shared spiritual heritage.

One particular evening, as they sat beneath the vast expanse of the night sky, the air cool and carrying the scent of the nearby fields, Isaac turned to Rebekah, his expression one of deep reflection. "Rebekah," he began, his voice gentle, "I often reflect on the journey that brought you to me. It was a path guided by faith, and it has led us to this place, to this life we are building together." He paused, his gaze meeting hers, a warmth radiating from his eyes. "I find in you a companion whose spirit aligns with my own, a partner in faith and life. This life we share is more than I could have ever imagined. I would never have thought that someone else could select a spouse for you who was a better fit than I could have selected myself. God truly knows us better than we know ourselves."

Rebekah smiled, her heart swelling with a reciprocal emotion. "Isaac," she replied, her voice soft, "my journey was guided by a trust, a certainty that the path laid before me was one of divine design. And in you, I have found a love that is as true and as steadfast as the faith that brought us together. This life, it is a blessing, a testament to the promises that were prophesied generations ago." She reached out, her hand finding his, their fingers intertwining as a silent affirmation of their shared journey.

The months that followed their wedding ceremony were not without their challenges, for life here in Gaza, while peaceful, demanded resilience and a constant reliance on their faith. Droughts would test your resolve. Not only did you have to solve dilemmas for your family and staff, but the neighbors and surrounding communities would also come to Abraham for assistance.

Rebekah had never seen a community that networked together so well. They shared resources and never complained about how much time they had to give or share with others. In every circumstance, they faced these trials together, their bond strengthening with each shared experience. Isaac found that Rebekah's calm demeanor and her unwavering faith were a source of immense strength for him. He smiled and thanked God each time he saw his wife help someone else.

Everyone was shocked by her quiet assurance, her simple yet profound trust in the Almighty, especially considering that she had been introduced to Yahweh by Eliezer when he met with her family. It had been so crucial to Eliezer that she would be willing to leave all of her family's idols behind in Ur and agree to serve the one true God of Heaven, Yahweh, the God of Abraham. She had heard the tales from the merchants of Abraham's miraculous life and how his God was always protecting him and fighting his battles. So, she agreed without hesitation!

"There are times," Isaac confessed one day, as they surveyed a portion of their land that seemed parched and weary, "when the challenges of this life weigh heavily. The responsibility, with its sheer magnitude, can be daunting. But Rebekah, we must remember one thing. Our God is everywhere. He knows everything that is going to happen before it occurs. Our God has us in the palm of his hands, where we are safe no matter what comes. We only have to prove our love for God by keeping our faith in him strong."

Rebekah placed a comforting hand on his arm. "But remember, Isaac," she said, her gaze steady and reassuring, "we are not alone in these challenges. The same Hand that guided me here, the same faith that sustained Abraham, is with us. We lean on that strength, and we trust in the unfolding plan. Even in the dry earth, there is the promise of rain, the assurance of life renewed." Her words were not a dismissal of his concerns, but a gentle

145

redirection of his focus, a reminder of the enduring power of hope and faith.

Their commitment extended beyond their sphere, encompassing the broader community of their people. They were mindful of the legacy they were building—a legacy rooted in the covenant and the principles of righteousness. Isaac, with Rebekah by his side, continued to honor the teachings of his father, living a life that reflected integrity, generosity, and a deep commitment to the divine will. Rebekah, with her innate wisdom and compassionate spirit, became a pillar of strength and encouragement within their extended family and the wider community.

The passage of time brought a deeper understanding and a richer appreciation for the complexities of their shared life. The initial joy of their union evolved into a profound and enduring love, one that was tested and refined by the experiences they shared. They learned to communicate not just with words, but also with glances, gentle gestures, and a shared silence that spoke volumes. Their lives became a testament to the enduring power of love, a love that was not a fleeting emotion, but a steadfast commitment, a conscious choice made anew each day.

Isaac often marveled at the depth of character that Rebekah possessed. He saw in her a spirit that was both resilient and compassionate, strong yet tender. She had a remarkable ability to discern the hearts of others, offering comfort and wisdom where it was most needed. He recalled a time when a dispute arose within the encampment, and it was Rebekah's gentle mediation, her ability to see both sides with fairness and empathy, that brought about a resolution. Her presence brought a sense of balance and harmony to their lives, a grace that permeated their interactions with all those around them.

"You have a gift, Rebekah," Isaac said to her one evening, as they sat by their hearth, the flames casting a warm glow on their faces. "A gift for understanding, for bringing peace where there is discord. You make our lives, and the lives of those around us, richer."

Rebekah met his gaze, a soft smile gracing her lips. "It is simply the echo of the love and faith that have been shown to me, Isaac," she replied. "And the desire to live in a way that honors that blessing."

The years that followed were marked by a steady accumulation of shared memories and a deepening of their mutual devotion. They navigated the ebb and flow of life with a shared resilience, their faith their constant anchor. The land of Canaan, which had once been a destination, became their home, the soil holding the imprint of their labor and the echo of their prayers. They were a living testament to the enduring foundation of love, built not on fleeting passion but on the unshakeable bedrock of shared values, mutual respect, and a covenant sealed by faith.

Their story was a quiet yet powerful affirmation that a life built together, in partnership and devotion, was a life rich in meaning and blessed by divine favor, a continuous unfolding of promises kept and futures forged in unwavering trust. Their journey together was a quiet symphony, each note played with intention, creating a harmony that resonated through the very essence of their shared existence, a testament to the profound beauty of a love that grew stronger with each passing season. The simple acts of their daily lives were infused with a sacredness, a recognition that even the most mundane tasks could be elevated by the spirit in which they were performed, creating a tapestry of shared purpose that bound their souls together.

The quiet hum of their shared life in Canaan had settled into a rhythm, a comforting cadence that resonated with the deep wellspring of peace Isaac and Rebekah had found in each other. It was in these moments of shared stillness, often beneath the vast, star-dusted canvas of the

Canaanite night, that their hearts began to speak the language of aspiration. The foundation of their union, built on shared faith and mutual respect, now yearned to expand, to encompass the profound dreams that lay nestled within their souls.

One evening, as the scent of drying herbs perfumed the air and the gentle bleating of their flocks drifted from the nearby fields, Isaac found Rebekah gazing out at the horizon, her profile etched in the soft moonlight. He joined her, his presence a silent question, and she turned, her eyes reflecting the starlight. "Isaac," she began, her voice a soft murmur, "as I watch the stars wheel across the sky, I can't help but think of the generations before us, and those yet to come. I find myself dreaming of the life we will build, not just for ourselves, but for those who will carry our legacy forward."

Isaac reached for her hand, his touch a gentle affirmation of her presence. "I understand, Rebekah," he replied, his voice laced with the same longing. "My father, Abraham, carried a vision that stretched far beyond his days. He entrusted me with a heritage, a covenant that speaks of a future I am still learning to grasp fully. And as I look at you, my heart echoes with the same desire – to see that covenant flourish, to see our lives become a part of that grand, unfolding story." He squeezed her hand, a silent promise in the gesture. "I dream of children, Rebekah. Sons and daughters who will bear the mark of our faith, who will walk in the ways of righteousness."

Rebekah's eyes softened with a tender understanding. "Children," she whispered, the word imbued with a profound hope. "Yes, Isaac. I, too, have dreamt of that. Of the laughter of little ones filling our home, of teaching them the stories of our fathers, and of watching them grow strong in their faith. It is a deep-seated yearning, a natural extension of the love we share. To see this love bear fruit, to nurture new life that will continue the journey we have begun." She leaned her head

148

against his shoulder, a sense of shared purpose settling between them. "I envision a home filled not only with the work of our hands, but with the presence of a family, a lineage that honors the promises made to your father, and through him, to all of us."

But I struggle with the fact that Yahweh had not given us children. I have been your wife for 20 years. Why is he making us wait? I am 34 and you are 60. Will God test us till I am 90 like he did your parents? Rebekah asked reverently. Isaac took her hand and pulled her close. It was his time to comfort her and show her the love he could give her. "My love, we will have children soon. I know it. Waiting on God is the hardest thing we have to do in our worship of him."

Recently, their conversations had shifted to children, unlike those during their early years. When they were first married, they talked about their travels and family histories on both sides. Things, acquisitions, blessings, and trading were common nightly topics. Then they began to share dreams and envision what God wanted from them. But in the past three months, something had come over both of them—there was this most unusual longing for children. So, all conversations eventually ended up on this subject. But tonight was different. There was a passion about Isaac that she had not seen before. There was a feeling inside of her that she had not experienced either.

As he comforted her and held her close, she wondered if tonight would be the night that would change history forever!

Rebekah tried to listen as Isaac spoke, but her heart swelled with pride and affection. The thoughts of a home filled with the sounds of children overtook her. She interrupted Isaac with passionately felt words, "I long to be a mother who instills deep-seated faith," her voice filled with earnestness. "To teach our children to listen for the whisper of the divine, to understand that our strength comes from a source greater than ourselves. I want our home to be a place where the spirit of hospitality, which your father so beautifully embodied, is a living practice."

The intimacy that grew between them was not solely of a physical nature, though that too was a sacred covenant. It was an intimacy of spirit, a profound understanding that allowed them to share their deepest vulnerabilities and their most fervent hopes. They learned to read the unspoken emotions in each other's eyes, to anticipate needs before they were voiced, to offer comfort and encouragement with a simple touch or a shared silence. This emotional resonance created a bond that was both powerful and tender, a sanctuary where their dreams could be nurtured and their shared aspirations could take flight.

Their discussions about children were filled with gentle anticipation and a trust in the divine timing. They did not demand, but they yearned, and in that yearning, they found a deeper connection. They spoke of the qualities they hoped their children would inherit – the strength and integrity of Isaac, the grace and discernment of Rebekah, and above all, the unwavering faith of their forefathers. They envisioned their children as bridges, connecting their present reality to the grand, unfolding future promised to their lineage.

"Imagine, Rebekah," Isaac said one starlit night, his arm around her as they sat outside their dwelling, "our sons and daughters, grown, raising families of their own. Imagine our grandchildren learning these stories and continuing the traditions. It's a vision that gives purpose to every task, every prayer."

Rebekah sighed contentedly, leaning into him. "It is a beautiful vision, Isaac. A testament to a love that seeks to extend beyond itself, to create something enduring. I pray that we will be wise stewards of this precious gift, that we will raise our children in a way that honors the sacred trust placed upon us. But when is this going to occur?" Isaac squeezed her close and said, "Soon, my dear, soon!"

The desire for children was a constant, unspoken prayer that underscored their shared conversations. They spoke of the qualities they hoped to instill in their offspring – a reverence for the divine, a spirit of generosity, a commitment to truth and justice. They envisioned a household where the lessons of faith were not confined to formal instruction but were woven into the very fabric of daily life. They imagined teaching their children the stories of their ancestors, the sacrifices made, the promises kept, all to foster a deep understanding of their spiritual heritage.

"I hope our children will be curious, Isaac," Rebekah mused one afternoon, as they watched the sheep grazing peacefully. "Curious about the world, curious about the divine. That they will ask questions, and that we will be able to guide them to the answers found in the scriptures and the principles of our faith."

Isaac smiled, imagining the scene. "And I hope they will have your gentle spirit, Rebekah. Your ability to show kindness even when it is difficult. That they will understand that true strength lies not in might, but in compassion and unwavering integrity." He paused, his gaze meeting hers, a profound tenderness in his eyes. "We are building a foundation, Rebekah, not just for ourselves, but for all those who will come after us. A legacy of faith, of love, and commitment to the divine will."

The emotional intimacy they cultivated was a testament to their deep compatibility and their shared vision for the future. They understood that the continuation of Abraham's lineage was not merely a biological imperative, but also a spiritual one. They were entrusted with nurturing a spiritual heritage, and in this shared purpose, their bond grew ever stronger. Their conversations were a delicate dance of vulnerability and strength, of individual aspirations and collective dreams, all underscored by a profound trust in the divine plan. They were partners, not just in marriage, but in the sacred act of building a future that would honor their ancestors and illuminate the path for future generations. The intimacy they shared was a holy space, where dreams were nurtured, aspirations were shared, and the future was envisioned not as a solitary pursuit, but as a collaborative masterpiece, painted with the colors of faith, love, and unwavering hope—a testament to the enduring power of a shared vision.

Isaac, too, felt the weight of this unspoken expectation. He observed his beloved, her outward composure belying the inward stirrings of her soul. He saw the tender way she interacted with the children of their household staff, as well as the quiet sadness that sometimes flickered in her eyes when she thought herself unobserved. His love for her was a fierce, protective flame, and he yearned to shield her from any sorrow. He would hold her close, whispering words of comfort, reminding her of the steadfast promises they held dear. "Our time is in His hands, Rebekah," he would murmur, his voice a low resonance against her hair. "He who has given us this covenant will not forget our hope."

Their conversations, once filled with the vibrant unfolding of shared dreams, now often returned to the themes of patience and trust. They would sit by the hearth, the flames casting dancing shadows on their faces, and speak of the faith of their fathers. Isaac would recount the trials of Abraham, the years of waiting, the seemingly impossible turns of God's providence. "He endured barrenness, Rebekah," Isaac would remind her, his gaze steady and full of unwavering conviction. "And in his season, the promise was fulfilled beyond all expectation. Our faith is not built on immediate answers, but on the faithfulness of the One who answers."

This period of waiting was not a void, but a crucible, refining their love and deepening their reliance on one another and their faith. It was a time of shared vulnerability, where the usual masks of strength were set aside, revealing the tender core of their shared humanity and their profound spiritual connection. There were days when the silence felt heavy, when the yearning threatened to overwhelm the quiet confidence they strove to maintain. On such days, Isaac would find Rebekah withdrawn, her gaze lost in contemplation, and he would sit beside her, offering his presence as a silent testament to his unwavering love and support. He learned to discern the nuances of her unspoken emotions, to provide a comforting hand, a gentle word, or simply a shared silence that spoke volumes of understanding and solidarity.

Rebekah, in turn, found strength in Isaac's steady calm. When doubt would flicker at the edges of her hope, his quiet conviction would banish the shadows. He would share his struggles, not to burden her, but to remind her that their shared faith was a collective endeavor, a fortress built by two hearts united. "There are times," he admitted one evening, his voice low, "when I question my worthiness, when I wonder if I am truly deserving of the blessings bestowed upon me. But then I look at you, Rebekah, and I remember the grace that has been shown to us, and my heart is renewed."

Their prayers together grew more fervent and intimate. They would kneel, side-by-side, their voices rising in a unified plea, not for the fulfillment of their desire as a demand, but as a humble request, entrusted to the wisdom of the divine. They prayed for continued strength, for unwavering patience, and for the grace to find joy and purpose in the present, even as they held onto the hope of the future. "Let our hearts be open to Your will, O Lord," their prayers would echo, "whatever it may be. Grant us the grace to trust in Your perfect timing, and to find contentment in the path You have laid before us."

The societal expectations of their time weighed subtly on them. In a culture where the continuation of a family line was paramount, the absence of children could be a source of unspoken pressure and quiet judgment. While their immediate community was loving and supportive, there were times when Rebekah felt the curious glances, the well-meaning but probing questions. Isaac, ever sensitive to her feelings, would gently deflect such inquiries; his quiet dignity and unwavering love for Rebekah served as a shield against any discomfort. He never allowed external pressures to dictate their internal peace. He often reminded Rebekah that their covenant was with God and that His faithfulness was the only validation they truly needed.

"Let them speak their minds, Rebekah," he would say, holding her hand. "Their understanding is limited by the world they see. Ours is guided by the unseen, by the eternal promises. What matters most is the peace within our hearts, the knowledge that we are walking in His purpose."

Rebekah, whose very being seemed attuned to the fertile abundance of her homeland, experienced the stillness within her own body as a quiet, persistent ache. The gentle sway of the olive trees, the robust growth of the fields that Isaac so lovingly tended, all served as poignant, almost daily, reminders of the life yet to quicken within her. This was not born of restless impatience, but of a deep, intuitive understanding of her purpose—a maternal longing that felt as intrinsic as the steady beat of her own heart. She would often find herself observing the mothers.

One starlit evening, as they sat together beneath a celestial canopy ablaze with countless shimmering stars, Rebekah leaned her head gently onto Isaac's broad shoulder. "You know, my dearest love," she said softly, her voice laced with a newfound, profound contentment, "even in this period of waiting, there is a remarkable fullness to our lives. We have each other, a love that deepens with each passing day, we have our unwavering faith, and we possess the quiet knowledge that we are intricately woven into a story much grander and more significant than ourselves. Our lives are already brimming with purpose and meaning, even before the joyous dawn of our children arrives."

Isaac tightened his arm around her, his heart swelling with an overwhelming surge of love and deep admiration. "You possess a truly remarkable spirit, Rebekah," he responded, his voice thick with a profound depth of emotion. "You possess an innate ability to find light even in the longest, darkest nights. It is a gift, a testament to the incredible strength that God has so masterfully woven into the very fabric of your being." He paused for a moment, reflecting on the entirety of their shared journey thus far, on the lessons they had learned and the growth they had experienced. "This period of waiting," he continued, his gaze fixed on the distant stars, "it has taught us the true, profound meaning of perseverance, of steadfastly trusting in a future that we cannot yet fully perceive. It has forged a bond between us that is immeasurably stronger than any earthly trial or tribulation."

Their story became a whispered testament, passed down through generations, a gentle reminder that even in seasons of apparent lack, with faith as their guide and love as their strength, the most profound and enduring blessings await those who patiently trust in the divine orchestration of their lives. They had found their fulfillment in the rich, transformative journey that had led them there —a journey marked by unwavering faith in a God who loved them perfectly and had a perfect plan for their lives. Their contentment was a quiet symphony, playing in harmony with the eternal promises of God, a melody of peace, purpose, and enduring love that resonated through the very heart of their existence. The reward of their patience was not merely a future blessing, but the profound peace and unwavering certainty they had cultivated in the present, a testament to the enduring power of faith in every season of life.

## Chapter Eight:

# *Love, Faith, and*

# *A Legacy*

The subtle shift in Rebekah's being was not a sudden storm, but a gentle unfolding, like the first shy bloom of a desert flower after a long-awaited rain. Isaac, ever attuned to her slightest nuance, noticed it first in the way she moved, with a softer cadence to her steps and a newfound luminescence in her eyes that even the softest lamp could not entirely explain. Their shared moments, already rich with the understanding forged through years of patient waiting, seemed to deepen, imbued with a silent, expectant joy. He found himself watching her more intently, catching the faint blush that rose unbidden to her cheeks, the way she would sometimes pause, her hand resting lightly on her abdomen, a private smile gracing her lips.

One evening, as the desert stars began to prick the darkening canvas of the sky, Rebekah sat beside Isaac, their hands clasped, the familiar rhythm of their shared quietude enveloping them. The air was still, carrying the scent of the earth—a testament to Isaac's diligent stewardship—and the subtle fragrance of herbs Rebekah had gathered for their evening meal. He turned to her, his gaze filled with a tenderness that time had only magnified. "Rebekah," he began, his voice a low rumble, laced with a question he hesitated to voice aloud, "is there something… different? Something more than the usual quiet peace we share?"

Rebekah's smile widened, a slow, radiant bloom that illuminated her face. She didn't answer immediately, allowing the unspoken to hang in the air, a sacred prelude to the words she was about to share. Her fingers tightened around his, and she leaned closer, her voice barely a whisper, yet carrying the weight of a thousand whispered prayers finally answered. "Isaac," she said, her eyes shining with unshed tears, tears not of sorrow, but of an overflowing, heart-shattering joy, "I believe… I believe the Lord has finally blessed us beyond our asking."

The words hung in the air, potent and transformative. Isaac's breath caught in his throat. He searched her face, his expression a mirror of her profound emotion. The years of anticipation, the quiet longing, the unwavering faith that had sustained them through seasons of unanswered petitions – it all coalesced into this single, breathtaking moment. He felt a tremor run through him, a wave of overwhelming gratitude that threatened to unmoor him from the solid ground of his being. He, who had learned to find contentment in their present blessings, now felt the stirring of a deeper, more profound fulfillment, a promise of life blossoming within the very core of their shared existence.

"Are you certain, my love?" he asked, his voice thick with emotion. It was not a question of doubt, but of awe, of a disbelief that such a cherished dream was finally within their grasp. Rebekah nodded, her gaze unwavering. "I am certain, Isaac. My body bears witness to it. And my spirit rejoices." She placed his hand over her heart, and he could feel its steady, rhythmic beat, a song of life already beginning its sacred melody. Then, with a grace that spoke of a deep inner knowing, she gently guided his hand to rest upon her abdomen.

In that touch, Isaac felt a connection that transcended the physical. It was a communion of souls, a tangible link to the future they had so ardently prayed for, a future now taking root within the woman he loved more than life itself. He closed his eyes, the image of their future, once a distant star, now a warm, nascent light blooming in the darkness. He felt a profound sense of reverence, a deep humility washing over him. This was not merely a personal triumph, but a divine affirmation, a testament to the faithfulness of their God, who had heard their prayers and answered them in His perfect time.

"Oh, Rebekah," he breathed, his voice choked with emotion. He pulled her into a close embrace, holding her as if she were the most precious treasure in all of creation. Tears streamed down his face, tears of pure, unadulterated joy and thankfulness. He held her close, feeling the gentle curve of her form, the life stirring within her, and his heart swelled with a love that seemed to have no bounds. He whispered her name, again and again, each utterance a silent prayer of thanksgiving.

It had been a twenty-year wait for Rebekah to conceive a child. It had been a struggle that Isaac had watched his parents deal with—so he knew not to doubt God's promises!

The stillness of the night was broken only by the soft sounds of their shared emotion. They sat there for a long time, wrapped in each other's arms, the world outside fading into insignificance. This moment was their sanctuary, a sacred space where their deepest desires had finally found their earthly manifestation. The years of waiting, the quiet resilience they had cultivated, the unwavering faith that had been their constant companion—it had all led to this. It was the fruit of their patience, a testament to the power of holding fast to hope, even when the path seemed shrouded in uncertainty.

Rebekah, her head resting on Isaac's shoulder, spoke softly. "Remember, Isaac, how we used to pray, not for a specific time, but for God's will to be done? How did we surrender our desires to His perfect plan?" Isaac nodded, his lips brushing against her hair. "I remember, my love. And how it felt like an eternity sometimes. But you, your unwavering faith, always reminded me that His timing is perfect, even when we cannot understand it."

"And your steadfastness, Isaac," she replied, her voice warm with affection. "Your quiet strength has been my anchor. You never wavered, even when my spirit felt weak. You were always the one to remind me that the dawn would come."

Their conversation flowed, a gentle stream of shared memories and affirmations. They spoke of the lessons learned during those long seasons of waiting – the deepening of their trust, the refinement of their characters, the strengthening of their bond. They acknowledged the moments of doubt that had surely touched them, but emphasized how their shared faith and mutual encouragement had always pulled them back from the brink. This was not a celebration of overcoming hardship, but a profound recognition of how hardship, when met with faith, could forge something even more beautiful and resilient.

The understanding that had always existed between them now reached a new depth. Their love, already a powerful force, was now infused with the miraculous promise of new life. It was a love that had been tested, tempered, and ultimately, deepened by the divine orchestration of their lives. The anticipation of a child, once a solitary yearning, was now a shared symphony, a harmonious blend of their hopes and dreams, woven together by the grace of God.

As the night wore on, Isaac's thoughts turned to the responsibility that now lay before them, a responsibility he embraced with a heart full of eagerness and a profound sense of purpose. He knew that the journey ahead would bring its own unique set of challenges and joys, but he faced it with unshakeable faith, knowing that they were not alone. They were a team, bound by love and devotion, and now, by the precious gift of a new life.

Rebekah, feeling his quiet contemplation, squeezed his hand. "It is a precious gift, Isaac. And we will cherish it, and nurture it, just as we have nurtured our love and our faith."

He looked at her, his heart overflowing. "We will, my love. Together. And we will raise this child in the knowledge of God's enduring love, teaching them the same faith that has guided us."

The quiet of their home now held a new resonance, a sacred hum of expectation. The absence that had once been felt was now a fertile ground, ready to receive the seed of a new generation. Their lives, which had already been filled with blessings, were now poised to expand, to encompass the profound and transformative experience of parenthood. This was the fruit of their patience, a tangible manifestation of their unwavering trust in the divine plan.

The narrative of Isaac and Rebekah was not merely a story of a couple longing for children; it was a profound testament to the enduring power of faith in the face of prolonged anticipation. It illustrated that patience is not a passive resignation, but an active cultivation of hope —a steadfast belief in the unseen and a deep trust in the ultimate goodness of the divine plan.

Their story, as it continued to unfold, would serve as a beacon for others, a gentle reminder that the most cherished blessings often arrive after seasons of faithful perseverance, and that the journey of faith is, in itself, a profound and beautiful reward. The knowledge that a new life was growing within Rebekah brought with it a wave of gratitude so profound that it seemed to ripple through the very fabric of their existence, solidifying their bond and deepening their reliance on the One who had orchestrated this miracle. The quiet waiting had ended, and the season of joyful expectation had begun, a testament to the unfailing love and perfect timing of their heavenly Father. The whispers of their prayers had finally been answered, not with a roar, but with the gentle, life-affirming whisper of a new beginning, a profound confirmation that their faith had not been in vain.

The preparation for their arrival was not merely about gathering necessities, but about spiritual readiness —a conscious effort to imbue their home with an atmosphere of faith and intentionality. They prayed together, not just for the safe delivery of their sons, but for wisdom, discernment, and the ability to nurture these two distinct souls in a way that honored their natures while guiding them toward the overarching will of God. Isaac, drawing from the deep well of his own experiences and the teachings of his father, envisioned a future where both sons would understand the foundational principles of their heritage, where the strength of Abraham's faith would be a constant beacon, even as they navigated their unique paths.

Rebekah, in her quiet contemplation, sensed that these differences, which were already apparent, would become more pronounced as they grew. She foresaw moments of friction, of misunderstanding, of contrasting desires that might pull them in different directions. Yet, she also held a deep conviction that these very differences, when embraced and guided by faith, could be a source of strength, a testament to the diverse ways in which God's creation can flourish. It was a delicate balance, she mused, between allowing them to be fully themselves and ensuring they understood the shared foundation of love and faith that bound their family together.

Isaac often found himself reflecting on the multifaceted nature of God's blessings. The initial joy of a single child had been amplified beyond measure, yet it also brought a heightened awareness of the responsibility that came with it. He understood that raising children was not a passive endeavor, but a continuous act of guidance, of love, and unwavering faith. He prayed that he and Rebekah would possess the discernment to recognize the unique inclinations of each son, to nurture their strengths without overlooking their weaknesses, and to instill in them a love for God that would be their constant compass.

Rebekah, too, felt this deepening sense of purpose. She saw her pregnancy not just as a personal fulfillment, but as a sacred trust, a calling to cultivate two souls for a greater design. She was already learning the rhythms of their lives within her, the interplay of their movements, the subtle exchanges that seemed to occur between them. It was a constant reminder that even before they drew their first breath, they were individuals, already beginning to forge their unique identities. She envisioned them as two strong pillars, each contributing to the edifice

163

of their family's legacy, yet each standing with its distinct character and purpose.

As the days drew closer to their arrival, Isaac and Rebekah found themselves in quiet communion, their hands resting on Rebekah's swelling abdomen. The desert air, carrying the scent of blooming wildflowers and dry earth, seemed to hold its breath in anticipation. They spoke of the future, not with fear, but with a sober reverence for the responsibility entrusted to them. Isaac, his gaze fixed on the distant horizon, where the sun was beginning its descent, painted pictures with his words—of two boys growing, learning, and becoming men of faith.

"Imagine, Rebekah," he said, his voice a low rumble, "two young men, each with a spirit forged in this land, each with the strength of our fathers, yet each with their unique path to tread. One may be drawn to the open plains, the boundless sky, seeking freedom and exploration. The other might find solace in the structured life of the homestead, the quiet contemplation of God's creation within the bounds of our covenant." He paused, his eyes reflecting a profound thoughtfulness. "We must be prepared to guide them, each according to their nature, to nurture the flame of faith within them, no matter how brightly or softly it burns."

Rebekah leaned her head against his shoulder, her heart echoing his sentiments. "I feel it already, Isaac. Their natures are so distinct. One is so restless, always pushing, exploring the boundaries. The other, a gentler presence, seems to absorb and reflect, a quiet observer." She smiled, a hint of a knowing twinkle in her eye. "It's as if they are already teaching us how to love them for who they are, not who we might wish them to be. Our task will be to help them understand that their differences are not a division, but a part of God's grand design, each contributing to the richness of our family's tapestry."

The preparation had extended beyond the physical. They had sought counsel from the wise elders, who spoke of the delicate art of parenting, of the importance of acknowledging and honoring each child's individuality. They shared stories of brothers who had found strength in their contrasting gifts, of how one's boldness had spurred the other's caution, and how their combined efforts, guided by a shared faith, had achieved great things. These were not merely tales; they were blueprints for navigating the complexities of family, for understanding that unity did not necessitate uniformity.

"The Lord has given us a precious inheritance, Rebekah," Isaac continued, his voice filled with a deep gratitude. "A multiplication of the blessing we so fervently prayed for. It serves as a reminder that His plans are often far grander than our imagination can conceive. We prayed for a continuation of Abraham's legacy, and He has provided two sons, each with the potential to carry that torch forward, perhaps in ways we cannot yet comprehend." He turned to her, his gaze full of love and a shared sense of purpose. "Our role is to ensure they are grounded in the faith that has sustained us, to teach them the importance of righteousness, and to trust that God will guide their steps, even as they diverge."

Then the day of struggles arrived. Rebekah went into labor. The midwives were diligent, but complications arose. It was like the two infants were fighting to get out. One appeared to be in a breach position, and the other was apparently sideways instead of head down for delivery. Finally, one of the infant's hands broke through. A midwife grabbed a red cord and tied it around the infant's hand, so she would know which one came out first.

To the dismay of the midwives present, the other child was born first. In the puzzlement of the situation, the midwife scolded the infant coming out first, "You naughty rascal, you broke loose and got out past your brother. I can see the two of you are going to be in

165

trouble!" Then she laughed as she handed the boy to Rebekah.

Issac was so excited that he could not handle the tradition of the father staying out of the tent. He pushed past two of the servant girls and was at Rebekah's side, looking at his son. "Esau is what we will call you!" Then he grabbed the boy from his mother for a victory lap by the fire outside, much to the upset of the midwives! Rebekah began to scream as the second one came out. Isaac returned to see if it was a boy, too. "Jacob will be his name! Esau and Jacob! Oh, God has given us a dual blessing today!"

Rebekah's thoughts drifted to the future, to the potential conflicts and triumphs that awaited their sons. She knew that their distinct personalities would inevitably lead to moments of friction. One might be impulsive, the other deliberate. One might seek outward validation, the other internal peace. Yet, she held a steadfast belief in the power of their shared heritage, in the binding force of their family's devotion to God. "We must teach them to honor each other," she said softly, her voice resonating with conviction. "To see each other not as rivals, but as reflections of God's diverse creativity. Even in their differences, there must be a shared understanding of their common source, their shared heritage, and the overarching plan that binds them."

The discussions between Isaac and Rebekah were not just about the future of their sons, but about the very nature of God's providence. They marveled at how their prayers, once focused on the singular desire for a child, had been met with such abundant generosity, bringing forth not one, but two lives, each poised to embark on a unique journey. This duality was a constant source of wonder, a tangible manifestation of a God who delighted in exceeding expectations, who understood the intricate weave of individual destinies within a larger, sacred narrative. They were not merely parents; they were stewards of a divine unfolding, tasked with nurturing two distinct branches of their family tree, each destined to bear its fruit.

The demands of parenthood, while joyous, were also relentless. Yet, through it all, Isaac found a singular peace in Rebekah's steadfast presence. She was not merely the mother of his children; she was his confidante, his partner in every endeavor, and the very heart of their home. When the weight of responsibility felt heavy, when the unique temperaments of their sons seemed to pull in opposing directions, it was Rebekah's calm wisdom and unwavering faith that steadied him. He would often seek her out in their quiet moments, perhaps as the children slept, their breaths soft and even in the night, and sit with her, feeling the quiet strength of their shared life emanating from her very being.

"You are my rock, Rebekah," he would murmur, his voice low and filled with a gratitude that words could barely contain. "In you, I find my true strength." He saw in her not just a reflection of God's grace, but its very embodiment, a living testament to the enduring power of a faithful heart. Their marital bond was the bedrock upon which their family was built, a constant, unwavering source of support that allowed them to navigate the inevitable complexities of raising children. It was a love that had been tested, refined, and ultimately strengthened —a living example of commitment and shared spiritual values that enriched their lives immeasurably.

The years that followed the birth of their sons were a testament to this enduring love. Isaac watched, with pride and a deep sense of fulfillment, as Rebekah nurtured their children, instilling in them the same values of faith, love, and compassion that defined her own life. He saw how their home became a sanctuary, a place where God's presence was felt tangibly, a direct result of the love and devotion that Isaac and Rebekah cultivated. Their partnership was not just about raising a family; it was about building a legacy—a testament to the power of love that was rooted in the eternal.

There were times, of course, when the pressures of life felt overwhelming. The demands of their livelihood, the complexities of their growing family, the occasional disagreements that arose, as they inevitably do in any marriage—these were all part of the human experience. But in those moments, Isaac never wavered in his commitment to Rebekah. He understood that true love was not about the absence of challenges, but about the unwavering commitment to face those challenges together. He would often remind himself of the vows they had taken, not as a burden, but as a sacred promise, a guiding principle that always brought him back to the core of their relationship.

He cherished the quiet intimacy they shared, the unspoken understanding that passed between them. It was in the shared laughter over a simple meal, the comforting embrace after a long day, the gentle touch of her hand on his arm as they walked together, that Isaac felt the most profound fulfillment. These were the moments that truly defined their marriage, the small, everyday expressions of a love that was both profound and everlasting. Rebekah, with her quiet strength, was the constant anchor in his life; her presence was a perpetual reminder of God's faithfulness and His abundant love.

He found that his love for Rebekah deepened with each passing season of their lives. As they aged and their sons grew into men, a new layer of appreciation for the journey they had shared emerged. The vibrant energy of their youth had matured into a quiet strength, a profound understanding that transcended mere words. They had built a life together, a testament to the power of faith, commitment, and an enduring, unbreakable love.

One particular instance illuminated this truth. Esau, ever the man of the field, had been presented with an opportunity to expand their livestock holdings into a more distant pasture. The venture promised significant rewards but also carried inherent risks, including potential conflicts with neighboring tribes and the uncertainty of an unfamiliar terrain.

Esau, fueled by his characteristic eagerness and a desire for tangible success, was ready to commit fully. Isaac, while recognizing the potential benefits, felt a subtle unease, a whisper of caution in his spirit. It was Rebekah, observing the exchange with her characteristic keenness, who offered the pivotal insight. She listened patiently to Esau's enthusiastic recounting of the plan, then, with a gentle hand on his arm, she spoke.

"My son," she began, her voice soft but firm, "the land is indeed fertile, and the rewards are tempting. But consider not only the harvest, but the sowing. Are the roots of this venture firmly planted in good soil? Have you sought the Lord's guidance in this new territory, and have you considered the peace that must accompany prosperity?" She then turned to Isaac, her gaze conveying a shared understanding.

"Sometimes, dear husband," she added, her words carrying the weight of experience, "the greatest riches are found not in what we gain, but in the peace we preserve. Let us not be so eager for expansion that we forget the security of our present blessings, nor the quiet assurance that comes from walking in God's will, not our ambition." Her words, spoken with such calm conviction, resonated deeply with both father and son. Esau, initially eager to dismiss her caution as timidity, found himself pausing to contemplate the more profound implications. He realized that his excitement had overshadowed a crucial element: seeking God's discernment for this new undertaking.

Jacob, in contrast, often approached matters with a more deliberative and introspective spirit. He would wrestle with decisions, dissecting possibilities and seeking a perfect path. When faced with the challenge of mediating a dispute between two members of their extended household, a situation that threatened to sow seeds of discord, he found himself paralyzed by the perceived complexities.

He saw no easy solution, no clear way to satisfy all parties. He confided his struggle to Rebekah one evening, his brow furrowed with concern. She listened intently, her gaze steady and reassuring. "Jacob," she said, her voice a balm to his anxious spirit, "you seek to untangle every thread of a complex knot, expecting perfection in your approach.

But remember, the truest justice is often found not in devising the flawless solution, but in approaching each person with empathy, and seeking to understand the hurts that lie beneath the surface." She encouraged him to spend time in prayer, not for an answer, but for the wisdom to listen, truly listen, to each side. She reminded him that God's grace often works through imperfect vessels, and that genuine understanding, born of compassion, could be the bridge that spanned their differences.

Jacob followed her counsel, and through his quiet prayer and subsequent gentle inquiries, he discovered that the solution lay not in a grand pronouncement but in acknowledging the fears and aspirations of each individual and fostering a spirit of mutual respect. Rebekah's wisdom, in both instances, was not about dictating outcomes but about cultivating the right soil within their hearts, enabling them to receive God's guidance with greater receptivity and integrity.

Rebekah's resilience was a testament to her enduring faith, a quality forged in the crucible of her own early life. Having navigated periods of uncertainty and profound change, she understood the ebb and flow of life's challenges. This understanding translated into a quiet strength that served as an anchor for her family. When drought threatened their crops, or when rumors of unrest stirred apprehension in the community, it was Rebekah who maintained an unshakeable calm. She would gather the family, not to dwell on the anxieties, but to reaffirm their trust in God's provision. Her prayers during these times were not petitions for the removal of hardship, but for the grace to endure it with faith and fortitude. She would often share stories from their ancestral lineage, tales of Abraham's unwavering obedience, of Isaac's steadfastness, reminding her sons that they were inheritors of a legacy of perseverance. "These trials," she would tell them, her voice steady, "are not meant to break us, but to refine us. They are the fires that purify our faith, making us stronger and more dependent on the One who sustains us."

Her influence extended beyond the immediate family unit, subtly shaping the moral and spiritual landscape of their community. Her reputation for discernment and her unwavering commitment to righteousness preceded her. Neighbors and kin alike would seek her counsel on matters of dispute, family feuds, and even spiritual questions. She approached each interaction with a deep sense of responsibility, recognizing that her words carried weight. She never sought prominence, but her character naturally drew others to her. She was a living embodiment of the values she espoused, her actions speaking louder than any sermon. She consistently demonstrated integrity in her dealings, fairness in her judgments, and a boundless compassion that extended even to those who held differing views. Her home became a quiet haven, a place where solace could be found, and where the principles of love and faith were not merely discussed but lived out daily.

The depth of her maternal love was evident in the way she nurtured not only the physical needs of her sons but also their spiritual and emotional well-being. She understood that raising children was a sacred trust, a continuous process of guiding them towards their divine purpose. She recognized the distinct personalities of Esau and Jacob, and rather than trying to mold them into identical molds, she sought to cultivate the unique strengths within each.

For Esau, she encouraged his generosity and his connection to the land, while also gently urging him towards a greater appreciation for the spiritual heritage they shared. For Jacob, she nurtured his introspective nature, guiding him to channel his keen intellect and his deep capacity for reflection into a life of devotion and service. She understood the delicate balance required in parenting – the need to offer freedom for growth while providing the framework of faith and moral accountability. She celebrated their triumphs with genuine joy and provided comfort and wisdom during their stumbles, always returning to the core message of God's unfailing love and the importance of living according to His principles.

Her influence was also felt in the way she managed their household. It was a place of order and abundance, not through ostentatious display, but through diligent stewardship and a deep sense of gratitude. She instilled in her sons a respect for labor, a recognition of the blessings that came from hard work, and the importance of sharing their abundance with those in need. Her approach to hospitality was legendary, always welcoming strangers with a warm smile and a generous offering, reflecting the Abrahamic tradition of extending kindness to all. This practice was not merely a social custom, but a living expression of her faith, a tangible manifestation of God's grace being shared through her. She saw every guest as an opportunity to demonstrate God's love, and her home became a beacon of warmth and generosity in the community.

Rebekah's resilience and wisdom were not merely personal attributes; they were the bedrock upon which the family's spiritual strength was built. She consistently reinforced the importance of prayer, not as a perfunctory ritual, but as a vital lifeline to God. She would often initiate family prayer sessions, her voice clear and resonant as she led them in thanksgiving and petition. She encouraged her sons to cultivate their relationship with the Divine, teaching them to listen for God's voice in the quiet moments of their lives. She understood that actual spiritual growth was a journey, and that it required consistent nurture and unwavering commitment. Her faith was a living testament to this—a continuous journey of seeking, learning, and growing closer to the Creator. This steadfast devotion was the enduring legacy she was weaving into the lives of her children, a legacy that would undoubtedly extend far beyond her years. Her influence was a gentle, persistent current, guiding her family and those around them towards a deeper understanding of love, faith, and the enduring power of righteousness.

Their lives, intertwined like the very roots of the ancient oaks that graced their lands, became a living narrative of God's meticulous design. It was a story not just of two souls drawn together by affection, but of a divine tapestry meticulously woven, thread by thread, through seasons of joy and trials. Isaac, with his quiet strength and deep wellspring of faith, and Rebekah, with her discerning spirit and unwavering trust, embodied the profound truth that when hearts align with God's will, their union becomes a powerful testament to His enduring providence. Their journey together was a quiet yet resounding affirmation that, in the grand unfolding of His plan, true love—patient and steadfast—would invariably find its destined course, leading to fulfillment and a legacy that resonated with the divine orchestration.

The very fabric of their shared existence spoke volumes of this truth. From the initial, almost hesitant steps of their courtship, guided by the hand of Abraham, to the profound commitments that bound them, every season of their life together seemed painted with the indelible strokes of divine intervention. Isaac, ever conscious of the covenant promises, approached his union with Rebekah with a reverence that acknowledged the sacredness of their bond.

He saw in her not merely a wife, but a partner chosen by the heavens, a companion destined to walk with him through the unfolding generations. His love for her, a deep and abiding current, was nurtured by his unwavering faith, a faith that recognized her as a gift, a reflection of God's faithfulness to their family lineage. Rebekah, in turn, found in Isaac a steadfast anchor, a man whose devotion to God mirrored her own. She perceived in his quiet strength and his gentle spirit the very qualities that God had prepared for her, a man who would cherish her, protect her, and walk beside her in seeking the Divine's counsel. Their shared commitment to honoring God in their marriage laid the foundation for a life that would, in turn, become a beacon of His guiding hand.

The challenges they faced, though at times testing, served only to deepen their reliance on divine guidance and strengthen the bond forged in faith. The initial uncertainty surrounding the birth of their sons, the distinct paths their children began to forge, and the ever-present need to steward the blessings entrusted to them—all these were navigated not with humanistic pronouncements alone, but with a conscious and prayerful seeking of God's direction.

Isaac's patience, particularly during moments of familial tension, was a virtue that had been refined and solidified in the fires of his upbringing —a quiet determination to trust that God's perfect timing would bring resolution. Rebekah's discernment, her ability to see beyond the immediate, provided the wisdom needed to navigate complex interpersonal dynamics, always to uphold the principles of righteousness. Together, they presented a united front, not of unyielding rigidity, but of resilient grace, demonstrating that even in the face of adversity, the steady hand of Providence was at work, shaping their lives according to a perfect, albeit sometimes mysterious, design.

Their commitment to living a life of faith was not confined to private devotion; it permeated every aspect of their existence, influencing their relationships with family, their stewardship of the land, and their interactions with the broader community. The abundance that graced their household was not merely a measure of material wealth, but a visible manifestation of God's favor, a favor they understood was to be shared generously. Their hospitality, a reflection of the Abrahamic tradition, was a living sermon, an open invitation to experience the warmth and provision of a life lived in covenant with the Almighty. Each guest, whether a stranger or a friend, was met with genuine kindness that spoke of a heart attuned to God's love, a testament to the fact that their lives were a conduit for divine blessing. The legacy they began to build was one of integrity, generosity, and an unwavering commitment to the principles of faith, a legacy that would undoubtedly ripple through generations to come.

The subtle yet profound influence they wielded within their community was a testament to the power of a life lived in alignment with divine purpose. Their home became a quiet sanctuary, a place where seekers of wisdom and solace could find both. Rebekah's ability to offer counsel that was both practical and spiritually grounded, coupled with Isaac's steady, peace-seeking nature, created an environment where truth and compassion intertwined. They did not seek to impose their beliefs, but rather to live them out, allowing their actions to speak of the transformative power of faith.

This authenticity drew others to them, fostering an atmosphere of mutual respect and spiritual growth. Their shared commitment to raising their sons in the ways of the Lord, instilling in them a deep understanding of their heritage and a personal relationship with the Divine, was their most significant undertaking. They recognized that the greatest inheritance they could bestow was not earthly possessions, but the enduring strength and guidance that came from a life anchored in God's unwavering love and wisdom.

The story of Isaac and Rebekah, therefore, stands as a profound illustration of divine providence at work. It is a narrative that reassures us that even amid uncertainties and through the often-unseen currents of life, God's plan is in motion, orchestrating events with perfect precision. Their journey underscores the enduring power of patience, the quiet strength found in surrendering to a higher purpose, and the ultimate certainty that true love, when nurtured by faith, will invariably find its destined path to fulfillment.

Their lives together serve as an inspiration, a gentle yet persistent reminder that divinely orchestrated love stories are not merely the stuff of ancient tales but a tangible possibility for all who dare to trust in the Creator's meticulous design, embracing the hope that awaits in a future filled with His promise.

The quiet unfolding of their union, marked by faithfulness and enduring love, paints a vibrant picture of a life lived in conscious partnership with the Divine. This partnership ensures a rich and meaningful harvest, both now and for future generations to come. Their legacy is not simply one of survival or material prosperity, but of a spiritual inheritance passed down—a testament to the enduring power of a love that is divinely guided, a love that conquers all and finds its ultimate expression in the

176

perfect will of God. It is a story that whispers to the heart of every believer, assuring them that their journey, however complex, is held within a divine embrace, destined for a beautiful and purposeful conclusion.

Just as God had a plan for Issac and had a Rebekah reserved for him, God has a mate selected for you. He has them "held" in a place, enjoying a relationship with Christ, until the appropriate time for you to meet them. Do not doubt or fear. God's selection of your mate will be perfect—even when you think it is not. Humble yourself and wait on God!

"Isaac and Rebekah" by La Wanda Blackmon

# Epilogue

---

Considering this book was initially written in the 1990s, while I lived in the Middle East, I wanted to share the story of how this series began and what has changed in this manuscript over the past 30 years.

I was an energetic writer. My 29-year-old mind was full of ideas. I loved history and often found myself with a romance novel and a Coke in hand, except when I was at work. So, for me to write religious, historical romance novels was not a far stretch of the imagination of those who knew me.

However, during the first Gulf War and my years living in the Middle East, it was challenging to find a publisher willing to take on a new, unknown writer. For manuscript proposals, they requested the introduction and the first three chapters if fewer than five chapters were included in the book. If you had more chapters, you had to send half of your book. Several publishers I dealt with required the whole book. That limited how many of those types of publishers I dealt with.

I almost as many manuscripts started as I had finished. When things got tough during the war, I found it easier to take a handheld pocket recorder that used tapes similar to those of an answering machine recorder (remember those popular little devices from the 1980s?).

I then started recording the books. I planned to transcribe them later. Then I ended up at a hospital with one of those old Dictaphone transcription systems. It used the same mini cassette tapes as my recorder. However, with the headset, I could get clearer recordings. They were no longer using them and had piled them in a storage closet. I asked for permission to take it to my flat and use it. This revolutionized my recording process, reducing my recording time. It used an electrical cord, saving me the cost of a battery. I was recording so much that I was going through about $20 worth of double-A batteries a month (for 1990s prices, that was a significant number of batteries).

Then a civil war broke out in the area where I was living (after the Gulf War ended). I stayed behind to help stabilize the region. However, the Islamic radicals were not happy with the westernization we were bringing to the area. At times, things would get confiscated and destroyed. Especially writings and binders containing papers. Not all of the soldiers could read English. So, if it was in English, it was considered to be religious writings or Western ideas that would corrupt the women of the area. So, they would burn it.

I boxed up my manuscripts in boxes of gifts I was shipping back to the United States for my family members. I put a letter in there with instructions for my mother to stack these binders in my old bedroom at her house. She and Dad were so busy with the church, I knew she would never read them. However, my dad would. Years later, I found out that he read every one that Momma unpacked. When I got married and all of my boxes arrived, I found about eight boxes of stuff I had sent as cargo freight via air (from the Persian Gulf region to Pensacola, Florida) at the port. Then my dad claimed them for me and put them in storage.

After I sent out my binders containing the writings and books I used for research while writing those nursing books and romance novels, I began sending out the tapes. I was putting them in letters and mailing them. However, they never got to the United States. So, after a few test mailings, I realized I could not send the real tapes with hours of my work on them without a plan.

So, I began going through my clothes. I decided I would sew the tapes into the linings of jackets and lined dresses. I packed the clothes and sent them by Air Freight. When they opened the boxes (it was apparent when we unpacked them that they had been thoroughly searched, but they did not realize that there were things sewn into the linings of those clothes). Only the clothes on the top were shuffled. I guess God wanted these books to make it! But the story gets stranger.

I did not even find those tapes until this summer (2025). Momma never unpacked the boxes labeled 'clothes'. They were just stored. I was rummaging through old storage boxes and opening them to see if I could donate some items to Goodwill, and I found clothes with these dictated books on tape inside.

I have found numerous tapes of books that were never transcribed into the computer. I do not even have a recorder to play them on. I have notified the publisher of my find. They are going to try to find me one of the old dictation players used by medical transcriptionists in hospitals in the 1980s. Those are the tapes I used for the recordings.

Once they locate a system to play these tapes on, we will start sometime in 2026, the laborious task of transcribing those stories. These will be novels, but they are based on true stories that people I helped save their lives told me their "love story."

What I am telling you is this: If you like this series, do not stress out - there will be more. The characters may not be Biblical characters, but the stories will all be true— just names changed to protect their identities.

I had asked Momma about those tapes, and she declared that they never came. She claims she forgot that I told her I was sending them in the lining of clothes. It is a miracle that I found them. I am now praying that the Holy Spirit has protected those tapes and the dictation on them. The shipping date on the last box with clothes and tapes was the summer of 1995. It is precisely 30 years later that I am finding them!

Now, let us return to the topic of the boxes shipped from the Middle East with book manuscripts and my laptop. My parents had never opened them, so when my husband tore these boxes open in 2012, we were shocked at what was inside. I had sent so many writings and books home that I had forgotten about them. I sat and cried as I read all of those manuscript rejection letters again.

As I read and reflected, the Holy Spirit spoke to me. "Well, my child, you know your future. Regardless of the wars, I always hold on to what is important to me. As I lead, you will finish these books. For those who have already been written about but were rejected, I will open a door for them to be published. I did not give you all of this for nothing. I did not instill in you the love of history and the Bible, so it would not be lost. Have patience. The time is coming. Just keep writing. I am going to introduce you to some people who will change the way you write. You try to write like Max Lucado and Francine Rivers, your two favorite authors, but I am going to change your style—you have a message that needs to be preserved for the tribulation period."

I remember those words as if it were this morning that he spoke to me. It scared me so bad. At that time in my life, there was one word and one phrase that would send my heart rate to 150, make my mouth go dry, and a headache would ensue. I did not know why. I was a Christian, and I knew I was ready—but I thought this was fear. Later, I was to learn it was the anointing; I did not know how to harness it. That word was "Rapture," and the phrase was "being left to go through the tribulation!"

I became a nursing professor, and my writing for educational purposes tripled. I have published numerous research, nursing, academic, and JACHO prep nursing articles over my nursing career. My healthcare writing was blessed, but everything I wrote in the scriptural or romance genre was a total bust. Then something terrible happened, which became my catalyst for change.

The COVID-19 pandemic hit in 2020 here in southern Alabama. God changed my ministry by combining my writing with my sermon preparation. I have continued with the healthcare writing. Teaching nursing is my career. Education is my heart. But preaching is my lifeline. I love to preach. I love to fast and pray. I love to spend time with Jesus. I would stay in my war room all day if hunger and the need for a restroom did not drive me out. It has not always been that way. COVID changed that. Something took hold of me during that pandemic. I could not spend enough time with God.

I even found that my hobby of restoring antiques was taking a back seat to my writing. That was not me. God was speaking. I was having dreams and visions. The more I fasted, the more he revealed himself to me. The visions were so real. I would be transported to a place that seemed so real. I do not know how to tell you without sounding delusional. So, I will say—the anointing is a fantastic thing—especially when you let go and let God anoint you!

In the midst of the COVID pandemic, I ended up with three large Christian publishers competing for my manuscripts. They were each trying to convince me that they were the best. I did not know what to do. God had anointed, and I knew I was on the right track. But I went from receiving hundreds of rejection letters to these three companies competing for the same manuscripts that had been rejected twenty years before.

But, "God is funny!" (I love this phrase by Eli's wife in the TV series "The House of David" that came out on Amazon Prime Video in February 2025). When I was praying and asking God which one of the three to go with, He said, 'None!' That is right. God did not select one of the top three. He did not choose a company that I had never written to or heard of—God selected a company that I did not even know existed!

So, "God is funny!" He does not see what we see. When he tells us what he sees, we think God is old and senile or at least out of touch with the 21st Century. But if you can get over that fact and let go and let God, he will transport you to a place that you would have never reached, no matter who backed you! The center of his perfect will for your life and for what is coming!

Now, enough about how I got to this point with the writing. Let us talk about what I changed in this manuscript from its original writing date. I began writing about Isaac and Rebekah and Queen Esther when I was 21 years old. I wrote the introduction and one chapter. Then, in 1991, I added another chapter. Finally, in 1993, I had it basically written. But I started writing my new idea on Jacob, Rachel, and Leah (the next book coming out by HFT Publishing this year, with an eBook on Kindle). So, I never wrote the last chapter, which is typically the conclusion of a novel.

I had many historical details in mind because of my location in the Middle East when I last worked on this book. After HFT Publishing's unrelenting insistence this summer that I give them some Christian romance novels, I decided I had better do some more research and fact-checking. I decided to "Google" a few things to make sure I had them correct.

My historical information primarily came from the locals and scholars I encountered in the Middle East. Some of the things I wrote them were more myth than historical facts. That was the best I could get during a war.

So, I realized that I was not going to have to do very much editing on the first ten books to get them to press. The worst part would be the conversion from the 1990 Macintosh software to the Windows Office Professional 2021 software that my publisher used.

I immediately signed a contract in June 2025 for ten books in this series. By the time this book was finished in August 2025 and sent to the publisher, they had reviewed 31 of the manuscripts and accepted all of them. I have written approximately 50 romance books. The later ones have not been completed. I am not sure I will finish them. I feel such an urge to get this "Revelation Made Simple" series on the market before Christmas 2025. So, I do not make any promises except to say that there will be somewhere between 10 and 35 in this series over the next two years. HFT Publishing's goal is to put one per month on the market through the end of the year.

Read, enjoy, and write to me. Send a letter to me through the publisher, or email me at lawanda.blackmon@minister.com.

# Interesting facts

Isaac was 168 years old when his grandson Joseph was sold into Egyptian bondage. Genesis 37:14 Isaac was an eyewitness to Jacob's sorrow over the loss of Joseph and continued to live for 12 more years. Jacob was 108 years old when Joseph was sold into slavery. Abraham and Isaac died at the ages of 175 and 180.

When Joseph was 30 and raised to his position in Egypt, Jacob was 121 years old. At the age of 130 years, Jacob appeared before Pharaoh in Egypt. Jacob died at the age of 147.

Isaac was 75 and Ishmael 93 when Abraham died at 175.

Jacob and Esau (age 120), when they buried their 180-year-old father, Isaac

Jacob died at 147 and was embalmed and buried in Egypt.

When Jacob was 99 years old, Rebekah was 133 years old. That made her 34 years old when she gave birth to Jacob and Esau. Issac and Rebekah had been married 20 years when she got pregnant with the twins. So that would have made Rebekah 14 at the time of her wedding to Issac. Isaac was 40 when they got married.

"Isaac and Rebekah" by La Wanda Blackmon

The resources I used for fact-checking this series against the information I had collected in the 1980s and 1990s. These sites helped ensure that this Christian Romantic Novel matched the Old Testament Book of Genesis completely, with additional backstory elements added where needed to make the storyline flow consistently with the known facts.

---

The story of Issac, Rebekah, Esau, Jacob, and Abraham is well known. I took my interpretation of the following scriptures from the *King James Version* of the Holy Bible.

| | |
|---|---|
| Genesis 12th chapter | Genesis 17:17 |
| Genesis 22:8, 23 | Genesis 23:1 |
| Genesis 24:1-67 | Genesis 25:1-11, 20-26 |
| Genesis 26:1-35 | Genesis 27:1-46S |
| Genesis 28:1-22 | Deuteronomy 34:7 |

---

**Ages and statistics of the genealogy are explained.**
https://aish.com/isaacs-age-at-the-binding-akeidah/

---

**The following terms are defined below for your clarification.**

**Divine Providence:** The doctrine that God has foreknowledge of and provides for all things.

**Covenant:** A solemn promise, often established by God with humanity, outlining mutual obligations and blessings.

**Faithfulness:** Steadfast loyalty and commitment to God and one's commitments.

**Discernment:** The ability to judge well, particularly in matters of spiritual insight and decision-making.

**Stewardship:** The responsible management of resources and blessings entrusted by God.

# Websites

1) For the location of information about the history of Ancient Mesopotamia, the region, etc. I used https://bible-history.com/old-testament/ancient-mesopotamia

2) For lineage information on Abraham's family: https://thehistoryjunkie.com/abraham-and-sarah-family-tree-and-descendants/#:~:text=Abraham%20came%20from%20a%20family%20of%20pagans%20that,of%20Shem%2C%20wh o%20was%20the%20son%20of%20Noah, of Shem, who was the son of Noah.

190

3) History and info on Eliezer:
   https://chabad.org/library/article_cdo/aid/492
   6269/jewish/Eliezer-of-Damascus-in-the-
   Bible.htm

"Isaac and Rebekah" by La Wanda Blackmon

# About the Author

LaWanda Blackmon is an **ordained minister, missionary, and prolific author** with over 35 years of experience in ministry. She has authored over 25 nursing books and more than 100 workbooks in five nursing genres. She currently has two religious series in production: *"**The Redeeming Love Series**"* (a 60-book series) and the *"**Revelation: Made Simple Series**"* (a five-book series), before adding this 22-book biblical romance series, "***Love God's Way.***" As of the time of publishing this series, Mrs. Blackmon has over 122 books registered under her name (all genres combined). Most are still in print, published by various publishers.

Mrs. Blackmon has recently written three shorter books as an encouragement tool to help individuals who want to know more about spiritual warfare, but find it too intimidating. She began preaching at the age of 16, became licensed in 1991, and was ordained 15 years ago. Her heart has always been devoted to medical missions, both domestically and internationally.

Her education includes a two-year registered nursing training program, a double major (Associate of Science and Associate of Arts degrees), two Bachelor of

Science degrees (in Nursing and Liberal Arts), and two master's degrees (in Nursing and Education). Her doctoral work has been in medical research and education. Her work experience spans the full spectrum of nursing and nursing leadership, including consulting and freelance writing.

# Books in this Series:

Guaranteed—Contract already signed for these

1) **Issac and Rebekah**: *A Divine Love that defies all arranged marriage concepts!*
2) **Jacob, Leah, and Rachel:** Dealing with the Ultimate Deception while navigating *Two Wives and Concubines.*
3) **Abraham, Sarah, and Hagar**: *The love triangle that almost destroys a nation!*
4) **Hadassah**: *The Unusual Bride and the King*
5) **Hosea and Gomer**: *The Beauty of Redeeming Love*
6) **King Solomon and the Shulamite Woman**: *A Pure Love that Offers Everything*
7) **King Solomon and the Queen of Sheba**: *A Love forged in Wisdom from Two Worlds*
8) **Boaz and Ruth**: *Love the Second Time Around*
9) **Samson and Delilah**: *A Love that Destroys*
10) **King David and Michal**: *The Shepherd's First Love*
11) **King David and Bathsheba**: *The Unforbidden Love and Murder*
12) **King David and Abigail**: *A Love that Protects*
13) **King David and Abishag**: *A Last Love— Patient and Warm*

14) **Hannah**: *The Love that Honors a Second Wife*
15) **Ahab and Jezebel**: *An Unhealthy Love*
16) **King Jehoram and Athaliah**: *A Love that Destroys and Kills*
17) **Lapidoth and Deborah**: *A Love that Lets each other Grow*
18) **Adam and Eve**: *The First Arranged Marriage*
19) **Amram and Jocebed**: *A Love that Choses the Best Route even When it Hurts*
20) **Job and Dinah**: *A Love that Stays Regardless*
21) **Moses and Zipporah:** *A Love that Accepts You Regardless*
22) **Moses and Tharbis**: *A Love that was Fought and Forbidden*

The first five books will be put on Amazon as soon as HFT Publishing, Inc., has them ready. Three of these five should be available for Christmas ordering. The other two will be available by the end of the year.

Then books numbered six through ten will be available for 2026. They plan to have books numbered eleven through eighteen available for 2027 and books numbered nineteen through twenty-two available for 2028. All will be available to purchase from HFT Publishing in paperback format. Paperback and Kindle eBooks will be available for purchase on Amazon.

Although La Wanda wrote these books in the late 1980s and early 1990s, they need to be converted to the new, updated book publishing software. (It was not used back then.) This requires significant formatting and some changes. These books have never been published in eBook format. Also, new book covers are being designed that are more modern.

Of course, to ensure validity, all books are being fact-checked and researched by the editing department of HFT Publishing, Inc. to ensure that the "manually done" research in the 1990s is still valid and has not changed with 21st-century technology and artificial intelligence usage. It is impossible to convert the books within a shorter timeframe than 90 days for each book. The projected dates above reflect us having a 90-day window for each book.